SPELLS
and
SPANIELS

Familiar Spirits · Book 1

CHRISTINE POPE

SPELLS AND SPANIELS

Copyright © 2023 by Christine Pope

ISBN: 978-1-946435-63-7

Published by Dark Valentine Press

Cover design by Danielle Fine

Ebook formatting by Indie Author Services

From the Archives of Grace Bowersby, Salem Witch Archivist

It is a common misconception that all witches have familiars. In reality, nothing could be further from the truth. While no formal studies on the subject have been undertaken, most estimates calculate those witches with familiars as only eight to ten percent of the magical population, possibly less. A familiar comes to a witch when she is around nine or ten years old, and ready to take on the responsibility of having a magical companion. Familiars live as long as their witch compatriots, and generally depart this world on the same day their witches leave it.

Far, far rarer than those witches who have familiars are the witches who are able to communicate with these animal guides, despite not having a familiar of their own. In these cases, the witch in question can be called upon to mediate when troubles arise between a familiar and their witch....

Chapter 1

Keeping Mum

"AND WHO IS THIS?" I ASKED, EVEN though I knew perfectly well that the well-groomed cocker spaniel who sat at my feet was named Milo.

My latest "client"—I always thought of these witches as clients, even though technically they didn't pay me for my services, only covered room and board and any vet bills that might be incurred during their animals' stays with me—gave me a thin-lipped smile. She was a woman in her early forties named Darla Fitzgerald who lived in Chicago, and was probably the exact opposite of the popular concept of a witch. Her dark blonde hair was cut in a razor-sharp bob that just grazed her collarbones, and she wore a trim black sleeveless dress and high-heeled sandals.

True, witches didn't go around announcing their supernatural status, and worked very hard to blend in with regular society. Here in Salem, where I lived, things were a little different, just because our tourists expected the local witches to actually look like witches. Hiding in plain sight, my mother always liked to say, and I had to admit she was right about that. There weren't too many other places in the world where you could go walking down one of your city's main streets in a pointed black hat and a flowy black dress worthy of a Stevie Nicks concert without attracting some attention, but around my hometown, no one batted an eye.

Darla said, "This is Milo," and reached down to pat the dog on his head.

Maybe it was my imagination, but I could have sworn he flinched just the slightest bit before resuming his former stoic stance, standing at attention a foot or so away from his mistress. Odd behavior for a cocker spaniel, who were generally friendly dogs, and definitely a strange way to act for a familiar, who should have had a bond closer than blood with his witch.

Then again, if everything had been hunky-dory between the two of them, there wouldn't have been any reason for Darla to bring Milo to me.

"And the problem is...?" I prompted. When she'd called me to say she needed my help, she hadn't elaborated, had only wanted to make sure I wasn't working with any other familiars at the moment and therefore could give Milo my undivided attention.

"He stopped speaking to me," Darla replied. Her tone was brisk, almost no-nonsense, and yet I still got the impression she hated to admit such a weakness, to tell someone who was pretty much a stranger that relations between her and her familiar weren't what they should be. At the same time, it didn't seem to me as though her feelings were hurt, exactly, and more that she was irritated by the way Milo had thrown a monkey wrench into her carefully ordered existence. "It started about a week ago or so. No matter what I do, he won't respond to anything I say. That is, he acts like a regular dog and will obey certain commands, but there's absolutely no connection between the two of us." She stopped there before going on, now sounding urgent, "Can you help him, Ms. Hughes?"

"Charity," I corrected her, but almost absently, since now my attention was focused completely on the dog who sat a few feet away from me. He wasn't looking at Darla, and instead met my gaze squarely. His big brown eyes seemed almost imploring, as if he had something he wanted to say but didn't dare do so around his mistress.

If that was the case, then the best thing for me to do was to get her out of here so the dog and I could converse in private.

"I've never run across anything like this before," I said.

She crossed her arms. "So, you can't help?"

"I didn't say that," I replied. Something about this particular witch set my teeth on edge, and I told myself I needed to be polite. Even if Darla Fitzgerald wasn't exactly the most congenial person in the world, she was still upset, worried about why her familiar had stopped talking to her. My personal opinion about the woman shouldn't enter into the equation at all. "I'm only saying that, because this is a new situation for me, I can't tell you exactly how long it might take to work through whatever's troubling Milo. Give me a week, and I'll see what I can do."

"'A week'?" she repeated, now looking aghast. "I can't be without my familiar for an entire week! I'm buried in planning the Witch Olympics and need him to help out."

While I had to believe working as one of the organizers of the witch world's annual sporting competition would require a lot of Darla's time, I also knew that being subjected to such a stressful environment wouldn't be good for Milo at all. Something had made him go quiet, and I needed to make sure he was someplace where he would feel safe and relaxed. My carefully restored nineteenth-century cottage on the outskirts of town, with its large gardens and all sorts of friendly wildlife, was the best place for him now.

"I'm sorry," I said, even though I didn't feel especially contrite. "But we both need to consider what's best for Milo. It's completely possible it won't take a week, and obviously, I'll let you know if we have a breakthrough before then. At the same time, you have to give me the space I need to do my work."

A long, tense moment while Darla stared back at me, eyes slightly narrowed. Was she wondering whether she could get me to back down?

If that was the case, she'd be waiting a long time. It wasn't that I was the world's most stubborn witch or anything like that, but when it came to my familiar charges, I wouldn't compromise.

She must have read that determination in my expression—or maybe she was simply thinking she'd spent enough time in Salem and needed to get back to Chicago and her work with the Witch Olympics committee—but she released an aggrieved breath and said, "If that's what you have to do."

"It is," I said.

This exchange was taking place in the living room at my home off Winter Island Drive, since I liked to keep my two lines of work separate whenever possible. Most people knew me as Charity Hughes, the proprietor of Full Moon Apothecary, my shop over on Essex Street, but among the witch community, I was the "familiar whisperer," the woman who could come in and patch things up if the relationship between a familiar and their witch went sideways, for whatever reason.

I got the feeling Darla Fitzgerald wasn't overly impressed by her surroundings. Because I had animals coming and going on a semi-regular basis, my home had been designed for comfort and durability rather than high style, and I supposed the worn leather couch and reclaimed-wood coffee table looked hopelessly shabby to her eyes. Any woman who wore heels like that to a semi-rural setting obviously was much more concerned with style over function.

Or maybe, since she'd traveled here by broomstick, she'd figured she wouldn't have to walk any great distance. All witches could fly on broomsticks, although the speed at which they traveled depended a whole lot on their innate magical abilities. I'd never been all that good at it, although even I could take short hops around my immediate locale and longer ones when pressed. All the same, I had a very un-witchy preference for driving.

Many of us employed invisibility spells when flying so we wouldn't attract any unwanted notice, or restricted our broomstick rides to nighttime excursions when they couldn't be seen. A few months earlier, though, a few enterprising witches in town had built a drone with a witch figure attached and flown it around Salem, providing cover for those who needed to travel during the day but couldn't quite muster an invisibility spell to hide their presence.

Darla, as someone who worked on the Witch Olympics and therefore was expected to be proficient in such common spells, had of course been invisible when she arrived, and hadn't dropped the enchantment until I opened the door off the kitchen in response to her knock. Since my house backed up to Juniper Cove and I didn't have any neighbors to the rear of the property, there hadn't been anyone around to see her appear.

And most witches couldn't have managed to carry a twenty-five-pound dog on their broom with them, but again, I got the feeling that Darla wasn't "most witches."

She had an oversized bag slung over one shoulder, and paused to reach inside so she could pull out a large plastic bag full of dog food and hand it over to me.

"I only packed enough for a couple of days," she said, sounding disapproving. "I can send more along if you need me to."

"No, it's fine," I told her. "Just let me know what Milo eats, and I can get some more food for him."

"Blue Buffalo beef and brown rice," she replied crisply.

I knew for a fact that the local pet store carried that brand, so there wouldn't be any problem taking care of Milo's needs. "Got it."

Darla didn't reply directly, but only reached into her bag again, this time to pull out a well-loved stuffed hedgehog, one that looked as though it was about to lose its filling at any moment. "And this is Wubby," she informed me. "Milo needs him close by."

At the sight of the stuffed animal, Milo perked up for the first time, his big brown eyes brightening and his tail beginning to wag. Darla bent down and handed the toy to the dog, and he took it from her and trotted over near the couch, where he curled up on the rug and began to nose at Wubby in a friendly kind of way.

"And his bed," she added.

A large blue plush dog bed emerged from her purse, telling me she must have used a bag of holding spell or some other enchantment to fit it in there. After she set the bed down on the floor, she straightened and looked back at me.

"Well, I suppose that's it," she said. "You'll call me with any news?"

"Absolutely," I replied. "And I'll text you photos each day so you'll know Milo is doing fine."

Even that gesture—a little benefit I offered all

my clients—didn't seem to mollify her. Still wearing that annoyed expression, she went over to her familiar and patted him on the head. "I'll be back to get you very soon," she said. "Just remember, the sooner you start talking again, the sooner you can come home with me."

Those words sounded almost more like a threat than a promise, and I got the sense Milo felt the same way, since he didn't really respond to his mistress's comment, but only continued to chew on Wubby.

Darla's mouth tightened. "I'll leave you to it, then," she said. "I expect to hear from you soon."

Before I could respond, she strode into the kitchen, where she'd left her broom leaning up against the counter, then opened the back door. A second later, she was invisible, and, I assumed, on her way back to Chicago.

I turned toward Milo, who'd dropped his toy and was now staring at me with expectant eyes. "Well," I said. "I suppose it's time we got acquainted."

The first thing I always did with the familiars left in my charge was to take them outside so they could wander through the yard, could make their way down to the water. Since it was late May and everything was blooming, this made for a pleasant walk, the sort of ramble that usually got the animals to open up and give me some insight as to why they were having problems with their witch.

Not in Milo's case, however. Oh, he was clearly happy to be outside, and ran here and there, chasing after each new and exciting smell, but whenever I stopped and called him to me, then asked him a question, he just shook, tags on his collar jangling, and went loping off to the next point of interest.

Frowning, I followed along, figuring it would still help to be with him, to let him get used to me. After all, I'd told Darla this could take a week or maybe even more, so there didn't seem to be much point in putting pressure on the poor animal. Something must have upset him a lot for him to have gone mute like this, and even though animals —including familiars—were very different from people, it still seemed wise for me to sit back for a bit and allow him to open up on his own schedule.

Or at least, that was what I told myself. It had been seven years since I graduated from Salem State University and gotten my B.A. in psychology, but some of the things I'd learned seemed to have stuck. Some people might have wondered why I'd gone for a psych major rather than going to veterinary school, and I actually had entertained the idea for a while...until I'd realized my shaky math skills would never get me through all the science required for that kind of degree. They'd barely been enough for me to get a degree in psychology, and I'd only made it through by hiring a tutor to help me with those annoying-but-necessary statistics courses.

No, I had to rely on a local veterinarian to deal with any health issues that might crop up in the familiars I worked with, which hadn't been a problem at first. But then....

I shook my head and tagged gamely along after Milo, who'd now run to the water's edge so he could play tag with the little rippling waves that kept splashing against the rocky shore. This activity seemed as though it should keep him occupied for a while, which gave me plenty of time to stand there and brood over my current vet situation.

Doc Winston had retired about a year ago and sold his practice to a man named Noah Jenkins, who'd relocated to Salem from Boston. This in itself shouldn't have been a cause for concern, except....

Well, except that Noah Jenkins was way more distracting than I would have liked. Around thirty-three, tall, with thick brown hair and the most piercing blue eyes I'd ever seen in my life. More than once, I'd tried to tell myself it didn't matter what he looked like, that it was his skill as a vet which was important, but then he'd turn and hit me with those laser-beam eyes, and I'd feel as awkward and self-conscious as skinny red-haired me had been back in seventh grade.

Noticing that Milo looked as though he was contemplating a swim, I called out, "Not today, kiddo. I don't feel like having to give you a bath on your first day here—that water's murkier than it looks."

This gentle remonstrance made him shake a bit, as dogs often did when they were given a command they didn't particularly like. His response told me he didn't have any trouble understanding what I was saying to him, even if he didn't seem at all inclined to reply in kind.

He came away from the water and went trotting toward my herb garden, while I followed a few paces behind. At least Milo seemed healthy and fit, and very unlikely to require Noah Jenkins' services. As far as I was concerned, the less time I spent around the vet, the better. So far I hadn't committed any horrible gaffes, but I had a feeling it was only a matter of time before I slipped up and revealed how much his presence affected me...and that I just couldn't allow.

No, it wasn't as though witches were forbidden to fraternize with regular people. Actually, we had to be with men—or resort to other ways to get a man's genetic material—if we wanted to have children, since witch powers were handed down from mother to daughter. When those powers skipped a generation, as they sometimes did, then that daughter would be handed off to a nonmagical relative to be raised.

This all probably would have sounded extremely harsh to outsiders, but it was the best way to ensure our bloodlines remained as pure as possible, and that children without powers weren't raised around those who had received the witch gifts. Witches never had boys, so that wasn't a problem.

But I hated the thought that one day I might have a daughter who didn't inherit the powers that had continued through our line for hundreds of years, so I'd resolved never to get married and start a family. My family's blood would die with me.

Obviously, my mother had had a few choice words on that subject once I'd told her about my resolution to remain childless, and had told me more than once that I was borrowing trouble.

"After all," she liked to point out, "magic has never skipped a generation in our family, so there's no reason in the world to believe it would do that with a daughter of yours."

Maybe. On the other hand, I couldn't help thinking the odds must be piling up, sort of like how all the experts kept saying the West Coast was long overdue for an earthquake and was sure to be hit by the Big One any day now. Why take the risk?

At any rate, while of course I hadn't said

anything about how Noah Jenkins took my breath away pretty much every time I saw him, my mother had still figured out that I wasn't exactly indifferent to the man.

"It would be perfect," she'd proclaimed just the other day when we met for lunch at Red's Sandwich Shop. "You work with animals, and he's a vet. Some might say it's a match made in heaven."

"Some might say that," I'd responded. "But not me."

She'd given me an exasperated head shake, although, to my relief, she hadn't pursued the subject. And honestly, I didn't think she had much room to talk when it came to matchmaking. Witches married, of course, but they had to be very careful about who they allowed into their lives, since their significant others would have to be told about the witch world. Those weren't the sorts of confidences you could reveal to just anyone, and when she turned thirty-three, my own mother had decided the perfect man wasn't out there for her, and had taken matters into her own hands.

That's why I didn't have a father, except in the strictly biological sense. All I knew was that he'd been a student at Boston University and was blond and blue-eyed. A math major, supposedly, although I certainly hadn't inherited that particular gift.

I had a feeling my mother expected me to do

the same thing and hook up with the local sperm bank if I couldn't find my soul mate, but I had other plans.

Being alone suited me just fine...or at least, it did when it had been a while since I'd last been subjected to the devastating power of Noah Jenkins' baby blues.

How long my resolve would hold up around him was anyone's guess.

Chapter 2

Cone of Silence

Milo did seem a lot more animated when we got back to the house, which was exactly what I'd hoped for. And I didn't bother to try asking him any questions, only put some of the food Darla had given me in a bowl and then got out another bowl and poured water into it.

At once, the dog lapped it up greedily before launching into the Blue Buffalo meal I'd laid out for him. His tail wagged, telling me he was happy enough with his current situation.

Good. I wanted him to be relaxed around me, or I'd never get to the bottom of his current silence.

While he ate, I went over to the kitchen table and got my phone out of my purse. I'd set it down there after I got home from work, but I wanted to make sure nothing important had cropped up in my absence.

However, a notable lack of calls and text messages told me everything seemed to be calm on that front. My assistant at the shop, Sage Halloran, was another witch, a local girl who'd decided to work retail for a year or so before deciding whether she really wanted to go to college or not. I always tried to work with witches when I could, just because it was so much easier not having to watch everything I said in case I let something slip about the witch world that I shouldn't have. Also, since Sage was the granddaughter of Grace Bowersby, Salem's unofficial witch historian, she was another person who'd been around me pretty much since she was born, and we didn't have many secrets from one another.

Despite not seeming to know what she wanted from life quite yet—and who could blame her?—Sage was a great assistant, punctual and reliable, and also understanding about the times I needed to duck away so I could tend to whatever familiar I might currently have in my charge.

I didn't always have a familiar I was working with, of course. In fact, sometimes I had stretches of six months or more before a witch in trouble needed my particular set of skills to sort out exactly what was going wrong with her animal companion. To be honest, I enjoyed those times more than I probably should, just because it was nice to be able to focus solely on the store and not have to worry about rushing off to psychoanalyze a chipmunk, or whatever.

Yes, a chipmunk. Familiars came in all shapes and sizes and species, and, as far as I—or anyone who'd spent more time studying that particular subject than I—could tell, there didn't seem to be much rhyme or reason as to why someone might have a squirrel select them rather than, say, a cocker spaniel. True, animal guides tended to come in somewhat manageable shapes and sizes, because I'd never heard of anyone having a hippopotamus or a Bengal tiger as a familiar. Otherwise, though, there seemed to be an almost bewildering variety.

Done with his lunch, Milo came over to the spot where I stood, phone in hand, and gazed up at me. His tail thumped gently against the tile floor, as if he wanted to say thank-you for the meal even though Darla was the one who'd actually provided the food.

I set my phone on the kitchen table and stared down at him. Once again, his expression seemed almost pleading, although I still couldn't figure out exactly what he was asking for.

"Feel like letting me in on the secret, boy?" I asked as I bent down to scratch him behind the ears.

His tail wagging immediately speeded up, telling me he definitely liked the attention. However, he still didn't seem inclined to say anything, despite the way his mouth opened a bit so his tongue could loll out.

Except....

Milo hadn't simply opened his mouth to pant. No, it almost looked as if he was trying to talk, but couldn't for some reason.

"Is there something you want to say?" I asked, and at once, he bobbed his head, indicating "yes."

Well, that was a little bit of progress. At least it seemed as though he was willing to communicate with me, albeit nonverbally.

Because that was the thing with familiars—they were there to communicate with and lend support to their particular human. We witches still didn't know exactly why these animals sought out their particular humans and not others, and why they could speak with and understand one another.

Just as no one could quite figure out why I was also able to talk to familiars, even though I didn't have one myself. Growing up, I had a cat named Dia who'd been my constant companion, and after she passed away when I was in high school, I'd decided it was probably better for me not to have any pets, considering the way other people's familiars seemed to come in and out of my life.

But everything had changed that one day when I was nine and I heard Grace Bowersby's rat Jonah talking to her clear as day. I'd laughed at something he said, and Grace had fixed me with a very direct stare and inquired as to what was so funny. Then I repeated Jonah's little joke, whereupon Grace, who was a friend of my mom's and who'd been watching me while my mother ran errands, had taken me home and waited there so she could relate what had happened. Afterward, anyone in town who had a familiar had brought their animal companion over to the house to see if I could repeat the trick, and soon enough, it became very obvious that I possessed a singular ability no one else seemed to share.

No, I wasn't completely unique in the history of witchdom, but the last time anyone had seemed to be blessed with the same talent had been way back in the 1870s, when a witch named Matilda Evans had been able to do much the same thing. It had taken a while to dig up that particular tidbit, mostly because real witches like me and my mother and all the others scattered across the world didn't really have a central repository of witchy lore. Everything was passed down from mother to daughter, and sometimes the witches in a particular location would pool their resources to create a sort of informal witch library, like the one Grace herself had been adding to for decades, and yet nothing was really standardized or centralized.

Anyway, it didn't take too long for people to figure out that if they were having trouble with their familiar—it might start suddenly acting out, or sulking, or downright refusing to help with casting spells or doing other simple chores around the house—they could ask me to talk to the animal and see if they'd be willing to discuss their problems with what they considered a neutral third party. My mother wasn't thrilled by the situation, considering the requests started coming in when I was only ten years old, but she'd grudgingly allowed me to help as long as it didn't interfere with my homework.

"Did you want to tell me why you won't talk?" I asked Milo, and again, his tail thumped against the floor.

All right, then. Since he seemed fine where we were, I didn't try to coax him into the living room so I could sit down while we spoke. Besides, the kitchen was generally a dog's favorite room in the house, which meant we should stay put. I always kept some treats in the pantry for occasions like this, and I hoped I'd have a reason to reward Milo for his input before too much time had passed.

"Is it something to do with Darla?"

For a moment, the dog didn't look as though he wanted to respond to my question. His tail went utterly still against the cheerful, patterned cement tiles I'd had installed the year before, and his gaze shifted away from mine, locked on the empty food bowl only a few feet away from where we stood.

However, I could tell he wasn't asking for more

food. No, he was stalling because he didn't want to answer my question.

I thought I understood. After all, familiars were supposed to be completely loyal to their witches and never utter a word against them. My brief acquaintance with Darla Fitzgerald told me she wasn't the world's easiest person to be around, and I had to wonder why the universe had seen fit to provide her with a happy-go-lucky animal companion like a cocker spaniel. A cat or even an owl or raven seemed like it would have been a much better fit.

But since I wasn't in charge of such things, I couldn't do much to change the situation. All I could do was try to figure out why Milo was suddenly having such an issue with Darla after being her companion for decades. There was no hard and fast rule about when familiars came to their mistresses, but it generally happened when a witch was young, no more than nine or ten, or eleven at the most. And because I guessed Darla Fitzgerald had to be in her early forties somewhere, that meant she and Milo must have been together for decades.

What had happened to set him off now?

I hated to ask the question, and yet I also realized I couldn't leave it hanging out there.

"Was she mistreating you in some way?"

True, Milo looked healthy and strong and positively Westminster dog show ready, but you never knew.

At once, he shook his head, his oversized ears flapping.

Okay, I supposed I could cross that one off the list...or at least, I could rule out the possibility of physical abuse. Unfortunately, there were plenty of ways you could harm a living creature without ever leaving a mark.

"Does she raise her voice to you?" I asked next. "Call you names...ask you to do things you shouldn't?"

Milo shook his head again, only this time not quite so vigorously. Did his response mean there was a piece of my question that might have been a little closer to the mark?

I hesitated as I tried to think of a way to pursue that line of inquiry without causing the dog any more mental distress. Judging by the way his ears now drooped, I got the feeling my questioning had gone in a direction he didn't like very much.

Unfortunately, I couldn't just let it go. I'd told Darla I would try to find out what was going on with her familiar—even though I didn't care for the woman herself very much—and that meant I needed to ask again.

"Has she ever made you do something as her familiar that made you uncomfortable?"

Milo let out a whine and sank down to the

floor so he was lying on all fours, his chin between his front paws. It seemed pretty clear to me he was unhappy, although I didn't know for sure whether that was because of something his mistress had done or because he just wanted me to leave him alone so he could digest his lunch in peace.

Well, at the very least, I could show him I was ready to be his friend.

I lowered myself to the floor and sat cross-legged a foot or so away from him, glad that I'd recently mopped and therefore I shouldn't get too much dirt on the skirt of my black dress. Because we were coming up on Memorial Day, this partic-ular dress was sleeveless, but overall, my attire didn't change too much from season to season. There was no unwritten law that witches had to dress in black, but I had to admit sticking to a monochromatic color scheme made it a lot easier to choose what I was going to wear any particular day.

Even though we were already a little bit acquainted, I still held out a hand for Milo to sniff, to let him know I didn't mean him any harm and I wasn't about to make any threatening gestures. He ran his nose over my fingers and then got up from his prone stance so he could settle himself in my lap.

Well, cocker spaniels were known to be very friendly dogs.

I ran my hand over his head and ruffled his

oversized ears. Although I'd worked with several dogs in the past, this was my first cocker, and I had to admit I was already falling a little in love with his soulful eyes and obviously sweet disposition.

Exactly what had Darla Fitzgerald done to make him so depressed?

Because, even though I definitely wasn't psychic, a gut feeling told me all of Milo's current malaise had something to do with his mistress. After I was done comforting the dog, I'd have to do a little investigating about the woman herself and see if there was anything that leaped out at me as obviously wrong in some way.

For now, though, I just sat there on the floor of my kitchen, my canine charge in my lap, and hoped I'd be able to get to the bottom of the puzzle sooner rather than later.

Chapter 3

I Put a Spell on You

THE DOG ACTUALLY FELL ASLEEP FOR A while, just enough out of reach from where I'd left my phone on the kitchen table that I couldn't do much more than sit and wait until he was ready to wake up. In a way, that was fine, just because remaining still and quiet gave me a chance to connect further with Milo, to give him the reassurance I could tell he desperately needed.

Had Darla Fitzgerald ever sat with him like this?

Part of me wanted to say no, that the starchy, impeccably dressed woman I'd met only a few hours earlier would never let herself unbend enough to adopt such a posture, especially one that might require her to sit on a hard floor in one of her designer outfits.

Then again, people's public faces were often

very different from the ones they showed their pets. Darla could have been very affectionate with her familiar when they were alone together, although nothing in the way she'd treated the dog when she dropped him off seemed to indicate she was capable of that kind of behavior.

No one else who'd brought a familiar to me so I could work with them had acted remotely like that. They'd been worried, sure, even frustrated, but their affection for their animal companions had been obvious. I'd never experienced even the smallest qualm about handing them back over once I'd worked out whatever little hiccup might have been interfering with their relationship with their witches, but in Milo's case, I wasn't sure I liked the idea of returning the dog to his mistress when—or if—I was finally able to work through what was troubling him.

He deserved better than Darla Fitzgerald.

I released a sigh, one small enough that it wouldn't disturb the dog sleeping in my lap. He was breathing deeply, not quite snoring, and I knew he needed his rest. Yes, I was itching to get up and reach for my phone, or head into my office so I could power up my laptop and do a deep dive on all things Darla Fitzgerald, but for now, I told myself to sit quietly, even as I could feel one of my feet start to go to sleep.

Oh, well.

We sat like that for a good half-hour or so, and then he finally stirred, shook himself, and climbed off me so he could go get a drink of water.

I climbed painfully to my feet, doing my best to ignore the pins and needles that started to stab at the arch of my left foot. It would sort itself out soon enough, but in the meantime, I had work to do.

My phone had remained quiet the whole time, which I'd expected. Sage would only call in case of an emergency, and although Salem was busy most times of the year except during the dreaded post-holidays lull in January, I doubted she would be so swamped at the store that she couldn't manage until closing time at five.

Cell phone in one hand, I headed to the down-stairs bedroom I used as my office. The house wasn't too big—just a hair under eighteen hundred square feet—and had two bedrooms and one bath-room upstairs, and the third bedroom and other bath on the ground floor. Probably, it had been much smaller when it was first built in the 1820s, but the place had been remodeled enough times that it was impossible to guess exactly what its orig-inal footprint might have been. I probably hadn't helped much in that department, since one of my first projects after I bought the house was to knock down the wall between the kitchen and the dining room and open it up as much as possible. Now light flooded through the entire downstairs even on the dreariest winter days, and my home always felt welcoming from the moment you walked in the door.

Milo padded along after me, obviously curious as to what I was up to now. His expression might have fallen a bit when I sat down at my desk and opened up the laptop that waited there, but then he curled up on the rug a few feet away from where I sat, nose on his paws, watching to see what I was going to do next.

The resigned look on his face told me that Darla probably spent plenty of time on her computer, too, and that, while he wasn't utterly thrilled about the situation, he also knew the best thing to do was wait nearby until I was done with my current task.

Which, at the moment, didn't involve much more than Googling Darla's name and the city where she lived, just so I could narrow things down a bit. And yes, witches used laptops and Google and cell phones and most other modern conveniences, just because it was a lot simpler to have an algorithm do the work for you rather than concocting a spell to dredge up the desired information. If this search turned out to be less than helpful, then maybe I'd try creating an enchantment to do the same thing, or even reach for the silver bowl I used as my scrying mirror, although scrying wasn't one of my top talents, and I couldn't always be sure that I'd be able to see something useful.

It didn't take much work to discover that Darla Fitzgerald was forty-one years old, had attended Northwestern University, and owned a public relations company. Lots of witches were their own bosses, so the fact that she owned a PR firm didn't surprise me too much. In fact, her position as CEO of Fitzgerald Consulting probably explained why she was on the Witch Olympics committee, just because there was always a lot of outreach involved. The event was popular, true, but it also involved some cajoling on the part of the witch community wherever the Olympics were taking place. While we always cast lots of enchantments to make sure we hid our activities from the mundies—mundane, nonmagical people—the risk still remained that hundreds of witches gathering in one place might attract the wrong sort of attention.

Anyway, on the surface there didn't seem to be much about Darla Fitzgerald that was terribly exceptional. Her parents still lived in Chicago, and she seemed to be single. I might have experienced just the slightest pang that her family seemed to be so normal, but I pushed the twinge of jealousy aside. My mother had done a great job of raising me and had made sure I never missed out on anything just because I didn't have a father around, and I knew I should be grateful to her for taking on the massive challenge of parenting a child on her own.

All the same, I found myself annoyed that Darla had done such a great job of making herself look like a normal, upstanding member of society. That was what we witches had to do, of course, because we didn't want the world to discover anything about our true identities, but still, it was a little frustrating to realize I couldn't find a single hook to hang my suspicions on, so to speak.

So far, it looked as though I'd hit a dead end.

I glanced over at Milo, and his tail wagged just a little, as if to tell me he was ready to get up and head out of my office as soon as I gave the signal. Because it didn't look as though Google was going to help me much more, I thought that was probably a good idea.

"Let's go outside," I suggested, and at once the dog got to his feet, tail now moving with much more enthusiasm.

This time, I knew him a little better, and figured it was okay to let him run where he wanted. My yard was fenced on all sides except the one that backed onto Juniper Cove, and since I'd already let Milo know I didn't want him going in the water, I trusted him to behave himself.

Which he did, trotting off to explore the line of oaks and pines that grew along the wall separating my property from the Davidsons next door, while I headed over to my herb garden, growing greener and lusher every day as we moved closer to the solstice. I always loved to walk along the neat gravel paths that separated the beds of rosemary and thyme and basil, all the beautiful plants that gave me the ingredients I needed to make the teas and tinctures and elixirs I sold in my shop. There were a few herbs that wouldn't grow in our northern climate no matter what I did to coax them along, so I had to mail-order those, but in general, I tried to work with what I had on hand.

The mint was growing so tall that I knew I needed to harvest it soon, especially when I realized it was about time for me to take another batch over to Stella Monroe at her shop, Tea & Sympathy.[1] She and her husband, a frost elf named Kai Ulfsen, ran the place together now that Stella's mother Valerie had decided to retire. Stella was expecting her first child, meaning she planned to sit out the Witch Olympics this year, but—

I stopped right there, thoughts racing furiously. Of course. Stella had been a champion broomstick rider at the Olympics year after year, and even though she wouldn't be competing this time around—probably to the relief of the other witches participating in the event, who would finally have a chance at winning the gold—she must have met Darla Fitzgerald during all those times she'd been a competitor. Maybe Stella would have more insight into Darla's character than I'd been able to dig up online.

A glance around the backyard told me Milo was still sniffing at the base of one of the oak trees. I left the herb garden and went over to him, then bent down to scratch him behind the ears.

"Come on, boy," I told him. "I have someone I want you to meet."

Stella looked a little surprised to see me show up with Milo in tow, but as soon as I told her I needed to talk in private, she'd turned to her husband, who was behind the counter at her tea shop, and asked him to take over. Because it was the middle of the afternoon, after lunch but before teatime rolled around, the place wasn't too busy.

Kai smiled at his wife, now very round as she approached the eighth month of her pregnancy, and said it would be fine and for us to take as long as we needed. I really hadn't expected him to respond in any other way, because he'd always seemed to be one of the kindest and most thoughtful men I'd ever encountered. Since I'd never met any frost elves besides him, I couldn't say for sure whether they were all like that, or whether

Stella had been particularly lucky in her choice of a life partner.

Because even though he wasn't my type...my taste seemed to run to handsome veterinarians with piercing eyes...I had to admit Kai was pretty darn gorgeous, with his white-blond hair, clear blue eyes, and perfectly chiseled features. Even his pointed ears hadn't turned out to be much of an issue, since Stella had cast a permanent enchantment on them to make them look like ordinary human ears.

She led me out of the shop and to the garden in back, a space with some wrought-iron tables and chairs scattered amongst bright flowers in tubs and with a couple of graceful birch trees providing a border to the enchanted little spot. One of the tables was occupied by a pair of women having a chat over tea and cookies, but they didn't spare a second glance for Stella and me, or our canine companion.

We sat at the table farthest away from the two customers, with Milo lying down at my feet. Stella smiled, asking, "Your latest charge?"

"Yes," I said. "This is Milo. His witch is someone who works for the Witch Olympics, so I was hoping I could pick your brain about her."

"Sure," Stella replied. "Who is it?"

"Darla Fitzgerald."

At once, Stella's features seemed to shut down. It wasn't that she exactly frowned, but more that the usual brightness in her expression dimmed. She was a very pretty woman with warm blonde hair and clear blue eyes, with the sort of casual gorgeousness that would have made her a good candidate for Miss America or some other pageant title, although no witch would ever have taken the risk of entering that kind of competition and putting herself on such public display.

"You don't like her?" I said.

Stella hesitated. "Well...."

I thought I understood her reticence. Witches generally looked out for each other, and we definitely didn't like to say negative things about another member of the magical community unless doing so was absolutely unavoidable. But in this particular case, Darla Fitzgerald had gotten my hackles up, and if Stella Monroe...who was one of the most easygoing people I'd ever known...had had a problem with the woman, then I needed to know.

"We're speaking in confidence here," I said. "I'm trying to figure out why Milo suddenly stopped talking."

Stella glanced down at the dog lying near my feet. His eyes were closed, and his tongue peeped outside his mouth. From what I could tell, he was having an awesome time just getting to lie there in the sun. I had to admit it did feel good to have it shining down on us, warm and friendly, filtered just enough by the trees planted around the outdoor dining area to keep the light from being too overwhelming.

Before she could speak, Kai came over, carrying a tray with two glasses of tea and a plate of butter cookies. At once, Milo perked up, his expression hopeful.

"Thanks, Kai," Stella said, smiling as her husband bent down to press a kiss against her cheek. "I should've gotten us something before Charity and I came out here."

"Oh, no worries," Kai responded, then bent down to pat Milo on the head...and place a small bowl of water next to the dog. "I thought you might want a little refreshment while you were chatting. Just let me know if I can get you anything else."

He sent a bright, friendly smile toward the both of us, then headed back inside the shop.

Yes, the guy did seem just about perfect in every way. Maybe I should have asked Stella whether he had a brother.

"It's some of your lemon tea," Stella said as I reached for my glass. "No caffeine for me for a while."

"Lemon tea is perfect," I replied, which was only the truth. I loved the tea's crisp, light flavor, perfect for a day like this—and a perfect accompaniment to Valerie's mouth-watering butter cookies. She might have retired from actually working at

Tea & Sympathy, but she still made all the shop's baked goods.

A quiet moment passed as we sipped tea and helped ourselves to a cookie. Milo sat up, tail wagging hopefully, and so I broke off a small piece of my cookie and handed it to him. There wasn't anything in the treat that would hurt him, and I figured the poor dog had earned it.

Stella wore a faint smile on her lips as she watched this exchange, and I got the distinct impression she would have rather continued to focus on the dog than redirect the conversation to the unwelcome topic of Darla Fitzgerald. However, since she also probably knew I wouldn't have come over here in the middle of my store's business hours unless I had a damn good reason, she said, "Something about Darla always rubbed me the wrong way."

"The 'wrong way' how?" I asked. "Did you ever see her interact with Milo?"

At once, Stella shook her head. "Not very much. Most of the time, she seemed to leave him at home. Maybe that was part of it—one of the other witches on the Olympic committee has a familiar, too, a pretty little owl. Artemis was at all the meetings I attended, while I only saw Milo once or twice. It seemed strange to me, since the witches I know here in Salem who have a familiar have them by their side almost all the time."

Well, that was true. Grace Bowersby always had her rat Jonah nearby, going so far as to have him ride along in her purse when she went to the grocery store or to have her nails done. To be fair, Jonah was very well-behaved, and remained safely hidden so he wouldn't startle a check-out clerk or Grace's nail technician, so his presence really wasn't a problem. And Isabel Hawkins, whose familiar was a gorgeous Siamese cat, also had Lita with her whenever she could.

The contrast between their behavior and Darla Fitzgerald's was glaringly obvious. Why would Darla want to keep so much distance between herself and her familiar? As far as I'd been able to tell, Milo was pretty much adorable in every way. In fact, if he'd been my dog, I would've done my best to get him certified as a service animal so I could take him with me wherever I went.

That Darla hadn't done the same seemed completely mystifying to me.

"Did she ever say why she didn't bring Milo to the meetings?" I asked next.

Stella reached for her glass of tea and took a sip, then shook her head. "No, she never talked about him at all," she replied. "Honestly, she kind of gave the impression that she was embarrassed to have a familiar in the first place."

That sort of attitude didn't make any sense at all. Having a familiar wasn't all that common, and the witches I knew who had an animal companion made it very clear they felt honored to have them in their lives.

But—as far as I'd been able to tell, which I had to admit wasn't much—Darla had done whatever she could to make herself fit into mundane life, to be absolutely the last person you'd ever expect might be a witch. Maybe having a cocker spaniel tagging along everywhere she went had required more explaining than she wanted to deal with.

Now that I thought about it, I guessed she'd attended Northwestern partly because she could live at home and commute to school. Having a dog with her in the dorm probably wouldn't have been allowed...and would have raised a lot of eyebrows, considering service dogs hadn't been nearly as much of a thing back when she would have gone to college.

Maybe Milo had simply had enough of her attitude, and had gone silent as a way of punishing his mistress.

As soon as that thought passed through my mind, though, I immediately dismissed it. For one thing, dogs generally didn't do vindictive things like that, were friendly and anxious to please. Even with Darla trying to shut him out, Milo would probably have done whatever he could to get himself back in her good graces.

And for another, even if Milo had been

freezing Darla out, that didn't explain why he wouldn't talk to me. If he really was that angry with her, one would think he'd take a certain pleasure in communicating with a witch who wasn't his mistress.

"I've never heard of a witch acting like that," I said, and Stella's shoulders lifted slightly.

"I thought it was really strange, too," she replied. "But since I was focused on the competition, I didn't say anything. Maybe I should have."

Her expression had turned worried, and I got the feeling she was giving herself some grief for not speaking up.

"None of this is your fault," I said quickly, wanting to disabuse her of that notion. "Especially because if you noticed Darla's behavior, then I'm sure other people must have noticed, too, people who worked with her on a daily basis and therefore would have had more place to speak up than someone who was only there to compete in the Olympics."

"Maybe," Stella responded. She sounded dubious, though, and I could tell she wasn't quite ready to let the matter go. "But I still could have talked to some of the other committee members and asked them if they'd noticed anything."

I supposed she could have, but I doubted she would have gotten very far. "They probably would have told you to focus on the competition," I pointed out, and she released a breath as she broke off a piece of her cookie.

"You're right," she said. "They're a pretty no-nonsense group of witches. I guess they have to be. Coordinating something like the Witch Olympics is a lot of work."

Although I'd never attended the event, I knew Stella was right. No, it wasn't as huge an effort as the regular Olympics, since the number of competitors was much smaller, but still, there were usually around a hundred witches competing in ten different events, with thousands more witches as spectators. Just casting all the spells it took to keep the competition a secret from the outside world sounded as though it would be extremely exhausting.

"Do you think any of the other committee members would talk to me about Darla and Milo?" I asked, and Stella shook her head again.

"I doubt it," she replied. "It's not like they're all best friends or anything, but they do seem to stick together, probably because they have to work as a group to get things done. They're not going to like admitting that one of their own is mistreating her familiar. If that's even what's going on," she added hastily, with a sideways look at Milo.

The dog, however, didn't seem to be paying any attention to our conversation, and in fact appeared to be asleep. I couldn't really blame him;

dogs slept a lot more than people did, and the warm sun and relaxed atmosphere definitely would have been enough to make him doze off.

"He doesn't look mistreated," I said, which was only the truth. His golden-brown coat was thick and glossy, and his teeth and toenails were in excellent shape. True, I hadn't performed a physical examination on him because that would have been awfully intrusive, but there weren't any telltales to make me think that sort of exam would even be required.

Stella reached for another butter cookie. "No, he doesn't," she said. "He's a gorgeous dog. But Darla seems like the sort of person who would do her best to keep up appearances even if she wasn't giving her familiar all the love and attention he needed."

My brief experience with the woman made me think pretty much the same thing. I could absolutely see her spending money on getting him healthy food and regular grooming and vet appointments, while at the same time not providing any real emotional support. And although I'd never heard of a witch treating her familiar so cavalierly, that didn't mean it couldn't happen.

But....

"We might not be getting the whole picture," I said slowly as I tried to puzzle through the conundrum. "There could be more here than meets the eye. I mean, why would Darla bring Milo to me if she knew she wasn't treating him well? The last thing she should want is some outsider realizing her bond with her familiar is a total sham."

That comment made Stella slump against the back of her wrought-iron chair. One hand went to the swell of her belly, so big that she looked as though she was about to pop any minute, rather than a month from now. "I hadn't thought of that," she said, sounding dejected. "But you're right. Someone as concerned with appearances as Darla Fitzgerald is wouldn't want anyone to know that her relationship with her familiar isn't everything it's supposed to be."

"Which means she only came to me because she was at her wit's end and didn't know what else to do," I replied. "Obviously, there are problems between the two of them, but I don't think the way he stopped communicating is directly her fault. Otherwise, this should have happened years ago, right?"

"You would think," Stella said, her expression looking as puzzled as I knew I felt.

What had happened? What was the breaking point that had made Milo retreat into silence instead of dealing directly with his mistress?

I reached for my iced tea and sipped from it

again. The liquid was cool and refreshing, but it didn't help my mental state all that much.

Too bad Tea & Sympathy didn't serve margaritas.

At my feet, Milo stirred, then looked up at me with hopeful eyes, so communicative on their own even if he couldn't talk.

Couldn't talk. Not *wouldn't* talk, as Darla had appeared to indicate. And in a world of magic, that probably meant only one thing.

As I bent down to give Milo another piece of butter cookie, it came to me.

I straightened, and stared across the table at Stella.

"I think I know what happened," I said, and she tilted her head.

"What?"

"Someone cast a spell on him to make sure he wouldn't talk."

---

1. To learn more about Stella and Kai's adventures, check out *Flight Before Christmas*.

Chapter 4

Dark and Deep

Because she was a witch, Stella Monroe didn't try to protest that casting a spell of silence on a dog was impossible. No, instead she crossed her arms and responded, "Why would anyone do that?"

"I don't know," I confessed. "But it makes sense. If Milo was just giving Darla the silent treatment, he wouldn't have any reason not to talk to me. I've only spent a couple of hours with him, but I keep getting the feeling he wants to communicate and can't. I mean, he can wag his tail and do other typical dog things. He just can't talk."

"Can he bark?" Stella asked, her gaze moving to where Milo sat at attention next to my chair, obviously hoping I was going to offer him another morsel of butter cookie.

"I'm not sure," I said. "I haven't heard him

bark, but that could be because he hasn't had any reason to."

Her gaze still fixed on the dog, Stella said, "Can you bark, Milo? Bark for us, and you can have another piece of cookie."

At once, he lifted a begging paw and opened his mouth. However, no sound came out.

My eyes narrowed. "That looks like a hex to me," I said. "Whoever cast that spell on him wanted to make sure he wouldn't be able to communicate very easily."

"But he can still respond to other things," Stella pointed out. "Can you nod, Milo?"

At once, he lifted his head up and down, and her blue eyes lit up.

"Well, at least he can do that," she said.

I had to admit I was feeling more hopeful than I'd been since Darla first dropped Milo off at my house. No, I still didn't have any idea why someone would want to keep the dog from talking to his mistress—or to me—but, on the other hand, he could respond to questions even if he couldn't elaborate on his answers.

"Did someone cast a spell on you, Milo?" I asked, and he bared his teeth, seeming to signal that someone had in fact hexed him.

His response seemed to be all the corroboration I needed. Unfortunately, knowing that someone had cast a spell to keep him quiet still wouldn't help me figure out who had done such a terrible thing...or why.

I also couldn't help thinking this was the sort of problem that couldn't exactly be solved by asking a series of "yes" or "no" questions.

"This is awful," Stella said. She looked just about as shocked as I was feeling, and I couldn't blame her. "We have to find out who did this."

"*I* have to find out," I corrected her. While under ordinary circumstances I would have been glad to have her help—we'd known each other since we were little kids, although our lives had pulled us apart over the past decade—there was no way in the world I'd ask her to assist me with unraveling this mystery while in her current state. She looked big enough to be carrying twins, even though I knew she only had one baby in her rounded tummy. "You need to take care of yourself and make sure that baby comes out happy and healthy."

For a moment, she looked as though she wanted to protest...until the reality of the situation hit her, and she realized she wasn't in any shape to be playing amateur sleuth at the moment. "You're probably right," she said, her tone resigned. "But maybe you should go to your coven with this."

My mother and I met with a group of other witches to perform certain ceremonies, such as the all-important ones at the solstices and equinoxes.

Ours wasn't any kind of formal body, though, just a group of like-minded women who found strength in numbers at certain times of the year. Otherwise, though, we all tended to go our own way, and while some of the witches in the group were very talented, they also tended to be pretty strong-willed, each with her own opinion on how things should be handled. I could only imagine the bickering that might ensue if I went to them with this particular problem.

"I'll think about it," I said, which was my go-to answer whenever I didn't feel like committing to a definite course of action.

Stella knew this about me as well, but to my relief, she didn't try to argue. "Well, maybe it's a good idea if you work on this by yourself for a while."

"That's the plan," I said. "I have a few things I can try on my own first. If none of them work, then I'll think about bringing in the big guns."

She glanced over at Milo. "What are you going to say to Darla?"

"Nothing," I replied immediately. It was entirely possible that the woman had nothing to do with the mean little hex that had silenced her familiar, but even so, I thought it better to keep quiet until I had more facts in hand. "I told her it might take me as much as a week to make any headway with Milo, so I've got some time."

"Oh, that's good," Stella said, now looking a little less tense.

Her response relieved me somewhat, because I'd only wanted to pick my friend's brain a bit, not get her involved with whoever or whatever had decided to make sure the dog couldn't easily communicate with anyone. I certainly didn't want to upset her, or worse, put her in any kind of danger.

"For all I know, it could be someone trying to play a nasty little joke," I went on. Although it appeared as if Stella was backing off from the situation, I needed to make sure she didn't feel compelled to pitch in. Making the spell or hex or whatever it was seem like it wasn't as big a deal as I'd first thought seemed like the best way to accomplish that goal, so I added, "For all I know, it's going to wear off sooner or later."

"Well, let's hope," Stella responded. "That would definitely be the best possible outcome."

After that exchange, we finished our lemon tea and cookies, and I thanked her for letting me bounce some ideas off her. She didn't try to stop Milo and me from leaving, or offer again to help, telling me that even if she didn't quite believe the reason for the dog's silence was as benign as I wanted to make it sound, she still wasn't going to interfere.

And thank goodness for that. I didn't know

where all this was going to end up, but wherever that turned out to be, I didn't want to drag an eight-months-pregnant witch along for the ride.

When we got back to the house, I let Milo roam around the yard for a while. I could tell he was fascinated by all the open space—the lot my house sat on was nearly an acre—and his response to my property made me think he and Carla must live in a condo or some other building where they didn't have much of a yard and where she would have to walk him several times every day so he could get his exercise and do his business.

As for me, I had business of my own to handle.

My specialty was working with herbs and creating a variety of teas and elixirs, although most of them weren't precisely magical in the truest sense of the word. However, I could whip up a decent potion when I needed to, and that was my plan now. Just a small, benign brew, something I hoped would allow me to see into Milo's thoughts and, I hoped, get an idea of who had cast this spell on him.

Other witches might have cast a spell of their own to ferret out the same information, but that wasn't where my strengths lay. Sure, I could use simple spells to make sure my locks never got picked and my windows never got broken—not that I had much need for such precautions in quiet Salem—or to make sure no one looked up toward the sky when I went on one of my infrequent broom rides. Invisibility still evaded me, so about the most I could do instead was use an enchantment that made people look in the other direction whenever I needed them to.

Pansy for thought, of course, and rue and mugwort and watercress. I didn't know how good the concoction would taste, but the beauty of a potion like this was that Milo wouldn't need to drink all of it, only enough to make a connection between us. I'd drink the rest of it...and hope it would be sufficient to open my mind's eye so I could see into his thoughts.

I'd just given the potion its last stir when the dog came trotting in through the kitchen door, which I'd left open for him. A simple spell kept bugs outside, meaning I could enjoy the fresh air without having to worry about any marauding mosquitoes or flies deciding to come in and make my life miserable.

Pretty much all my potion-brewing took place in my kitchen, although I also had a small workroom behind Full Moon Apothecary where I could whip up a special elixir if a client needed it right away. The kitchen at my house was a cozy, friendly place, with a large Viking stove and light quartz counters on top of pale sage-green cabinets, along with those fun tile floors to add a bit of visual interest to the space.

Milo came over and pointed an inquisitive nose toward the cast-iron pot that held the potion I'd just made. It actually smelled better than I'd expected, fragrant and herbal but not overly sharp.

"Okay, Milo," I told the dog. "We're both going to drink a little of this potion. It'll help me figure out who cast this spell on you. It doesn't taste bad, I promise."

His nose wrinkled slightly, telling me he wasn't completely keen on the idea. However, he didn't turn around and bolt right out the door, which had to be a good sign. Maybe he was reassured that I'd be drinking the potion as well, and therefore guessed I would have done what I could to make sure it didn't taste too nasty.

This wasn't the first time I'd had to dose a familiar with one of my herbal cures, although I'd never had to brew something to see into an animal's mind before this. But because of the parade of animals that went through the house, I had various sizes of droppers that I could use to give them some form of medicine.

I got out one and dipped it into the potion, which was a soft, rosy shade and looked very innocuous. Milo's dubious expression cheered up a little bit at the sight of the liquid in the dropper.

Possibly he'd thought it would be bile green or something equally unappetizing.

After filling up the dropper, I settled down on my heels so I could give the dog his dose. For just the briefest moment, he seemed to resist, his mouth staying firmly shut, but after I tilted my head at him and gave him a very direct look to let him know that potion was going down his throat one way or another, he relented and let me tip the brew into his mouth.

At once, he gave a shake, his nose wrinkling again. No doubt if he'd still had the power of speech, he would have exclaimed "Yuck!" or said something else to let me know the potion didn't taste nearly as good as it looked.

Which made me not terribly eager to drink the brew, either, but it wouldn't work unless both of us had consumed a dose. Besides, I'd told Milo I was going to take it, too, and there was no way I'd go back on my word like that.

No need of a dropper for me; I got a spoon out of a nearby drawer and scooped up some of the liquid, then popped it in my mouth before I could lose my nerve.

At once, I wrinkled my nose at the murky flavor. No, it wasn't the nastiest potion I'd ever swallowed, but it also didn't exactly taste like a box of chocolates.

But now that we both had the potion swirling around in our systems, it was time to get to work.

I squatted down next to Milo again and reached out so I could lay a hand on his head. At once, I was hit with a whirl of impressions—the kitchen we both currently occupied, with all its interesting shapes and smells, and more enticing aromas wafting in through the kitchen door from the herb garden and flowerbeds outside. My own self as viewed through the dog's eyes, surrounded by a kind of glow that made me look like some sort of goddess descended to earth instead of your usual garden-variety witch.

It seemed pretty obvious that Milo looked at me as some kind of savior. Exactly what had he gone through while living with Darla Fitzgerald?

"Can you think of the person who cast the spell, Milo?" I asked. "Try to picture them in your mind."

The dog let out a soft little chuff of a breath, as if to tell me he would do his best. Afterward, the image of me and my kitchen faded from his mind, and instead I saw a very different sort of space, cold and modern, elegant in its own way.

There was Darla, bending down to pour some food into a stainless-steel bowl in what looked like the laundry room of her house or condo. This time she wore a slim beige skirt and cream blouse and extremely expensive-looking lizard-skin pumps instead of the chic black dress she'd had on when she dropped off Milo, but she still gave off the impression of someone who never left her house without looking completely pulled together.

"I know Darla is your witch," I said gently. "But I need to see who cast the spell on you."

Milo shook at that comment, the tags hanging off his collar jingling a little. Then he tilted his head, and the scene I was viewing changed again. Darla was still there, only this time she knelt next to her familiar and had her hand on his head. Her lips moved and she spoke in a murmur, but I could still understand what she was saying.

Say not a word
Never be heard
In silence remain
Until I say "speak" again

My heart seemed to freeze up. If what Milo was showing me was the truth—and I had no reason not to believe him, as dogs were inherently truthful creatures and never lied—then it was Darla herself who'd cast the spell on her familiar.

I jerked away in shock, and as soon as my hand lifted from the dog's soft fur, the image was gone, the connection broken.

However, I'd seen enough.

Why in the world would Darla Fitzgerald want

to make sure her dog couldn't talk? It wasn't as though a familiar could speak to anyone besides their mistress...or to someone like me, but as far as I knew, I was currently the only person in the witch world who possessed that particular talent. And because I possessed that particular gift, I should have been the last person Darla would want around Milo...and yet she'd brought him to me.

None of this made any sense.

"Good boy," I told Milo, and rose to my feet so I could go over to the cupboard and get him a treat.

He followed me, tail wagging, and looked much more cheerful than he had a few minutes earlier. Maybe he was just glad that now someone else knew his secret and he wouldn't have to bear the burden alone.

As he munched on his treat, though, I found myself frowning. What was I supposed to do with the knowledge I'd just acquired? Confront Darla directly? Go to my mother for advice?

Problem was, I didn't know how much help my mother could even give me. It wasn't as though she would have encountered a situation like this ever before.

Well, I'd never been the sort of person to beat around the bush, so I figured I might as well call Darla and see if she could possibly offer an explanation that made any sense.

My purse sat in its usual place on the kitchen

table, so I reached inside and scooped out my cell phone. I'd already entered Darla's information in my contacts list, and that meant it took me only a few seconds to find her name and then touch the screen to connect the call.

It rang three times, and I felt myself tensing slightly. What if she was busy and it went to voice-mail? This wasn't the sort of problem I wanted to explain in a phone message.

But then a man's brisk-sounding voice said, "Darla Fitzgerald's phone. Who is this?"

"Charity Hughes," I replied, alarm bells already going off in my mind. However, I wasn't so shaken that I forgot to use the standard story I always employed to explain the way I watched other witch's familiars. "I'm pet sitting for Darla. Who are you?"

"Detective Adams, Chicago P.D.," the man replied. "A neighbor called in the sound of a gunshot, and we arrived on scene to find Darla Fitzgerald's body in her condo."

Chapter 5

Scene of the Crime

FOR ONE LONG, HORRIBLE MOMENT, I JUST stood there, my cell phone pressed against my ear. Then I stammered, "Are—are you sure it was Darla?"

"Yes," Detective Adams said. "We've positively ID'd Ms. Fitzgerald and verified that she died of a single gunshot wound. I'm sorry you had to find out this way."

"It's—" I began, then stopped. I'd been about to say it was fine, but of course, it wasn't. Not with Darla Fitzgerald dead half a continent away. "Do you—do you know who did it?"

"Not yet," he said. "It's still an active crime scene. I'm afraid I can't tell you anything more than that."

I'd heard enough, though. Someone had gone to Darla's condo and shot her dead.

Had she left Milo with me because she feared for her life and wanted him safely out of harm's way? If that was really what had happened, then she must have cared for her familiar more than her actions might have otherwise indicated.

Before I could respond to Detective Adams' comment, he went on, "You said you were watching her dog?"

"Yes."

"Did she say anything to you when she dropped off the animal, something that might have indicated she had any enemies?"

As best I could, I tried to recall all the particulars of our meeting. Darla had been brisk and not exactly what you could call friendly, but I'd just thought that was her usual manner and hadn't attributed any sinister motivations to anything she'd said. "Not really," I replied. "She seemed like she was in kind of a hurry, but I just supposed that was because she needed to get back to Chicago."

"'Back to Chicago'?" Detective Adams repeated. "You're not local?"

"No, I'm in Massachusetts." One would have thought he'd be able to tell I was calling from out of state based solely on my phone's area code. Then again, a lot of people kept the same number for years no matter where they lived, so maybe he hadn't wanted to make any assumptions.

"That's a long way to go for dog sitting," the detective told me.

Yes, it was. Thinking quickly—since I obviously couldn't tell him the whole truth—I replied, "She was having some behavioral issues with Milo. I specialize in that sort of thing, and that's why she brought the dog to me."

A brief silence followed that explanation. Was Detective Adams thinking of the best way to respond, or was he merely trying to figure out whether he could poke any holes in my story?

To my relief, though, he only said, "Got it. Are you able to watch the animal for a while longer? We need to notify Ms. Fitzgerald's next-of-kin, and things here might be a little chaotic for a while."

"I can watch Milo for as long as necessary," I responded at once. I might not have known what the heck was going on, but I did know that Milo was welcome to stay with me indefinitely.

Although I couldn't see the detective's face, I got the feeling he might have smiled slightly at my words. "Thank you, Ms. Hughes. My family has a golden retriever, and I didn't want to think of an innocent dog getting left out in the cold because of all this."

"Milo will be safe with me," I promised.

"Good. Is this the best number to reach you?"

It was the only number where anyone could contact me—well, except the one at my shop—

because my house didn't have a landline. "Yes," I said. "Feel free to call me whenever you need to."

"I appreciate that. You have a good day, Ms. Hughes."

Detective Adams ended the call there, and I set my phone down on the table, then looked over at Milo. He was watching me, expression quizzical, but he didn't seem too worried about the terrible fact that his mistress was dead.

His mistress was dead....

According to everything I knew about witches and familiars, those animal companions lived as long as their mistresses, and then quietly passed on almost immediately when their witch left this world.

But Milo looked just as healthy and vigorous as the moment he'd walked through my door a few hours earlier, which meant...what?

I didn't know, and couldn't begin to guess.

Time to reach out and get some expert input.

"You say Darla Fitzgerald is dead?" Grace Bowersby said blankly. She glanced from me to Milo, whose tail wagged just a little in response. "But...."

"Exactly," I replied. "I can't figure it out at all. That's why I came to talk to you—you're the expert on witches and their familiars."

"Well," Grace said, now looking a bit proud, but also a little ashamed, as though she wasn't sure whether she could claim the title of "expert" or not. She was a chubby woman around my mother's age, so in her middle sixties. Her curly gray hair perpetually wanted to escape the low bun she wore at the back of her neck, and she always seemed like the least witchy-looking person I knew, thanks to her fondness for brightly flowered dresses and tops. Even her winter sweaters were hot pink and lime and turquoise, as if she needed those vibrant colors to get her through the long New England winters. "I certainly don't go around calling myself an expert, but I have to admit the subject of witches and their familiars has always fascinated me, which is why I've studied it a good bit. Scone?"

She offered me a flowery pink plate with several luscious-looking pastries sitting on it. Even though I'd had tea and cookies with Stella only an hour or so ago, I knew better than to pass up one of Grace's famous white chocolate raspberry scones.

"Thank you," I said, and picked up the confection. A few feet away from the pair of armchairs where Grace and I sat, Milo watched this exchange and gave a hopeful thump of his tail, but I only shook my head. "It's got chocolate in it, buddy," I told him. "That's a no-no."

Now looking dejected, he settled down on the floor, his chin between his paws.

"He seems just fine," Grace said, still wearing that same puzzled expression. Her own familiar, the rat Jonah, was perched on the fireplace mantel, black eyes bright with interest. However, he was a very well-behaved little rodent, and knew to stay away from any food humans might be consuming. "I don't understand how that's possible."

I didn't, either, which was why I'd come to see Grace. "You've never heard of something like this happening?"

Her brow furrowed, deepening the lines on her forehead. "I don't think so," she replied. "But I have stacks and stacks of notes, so I suppose it's possible I wrote down an anecdote along these lines and just can't remember." She paused there while she reached for the teacup that sat on the small marble-topped table next to her. "Do you—do you know when it happened?"

Her voice had dropped a little as she asked the question, and there was no doubt in my mind as to what she meant by "it."

"Not really," I said. "I mean, it must have been not long after Darla returned to Chicago. She went by broomstick and I got the feeling she was a fast rider, so the trip shouldn't have taken her much more than a half hour or forty-five minutes at the most. But the detective I talked to didn't give me many details."

"No, I suppose he wouldn't," Grace remarked,

sounding a little disapproving and giving the impression she thought Detective Adams should have revealed everything he knew about the case, even though doing so would have violated every law enforcement guideline I'd ever heard of. "But you definitely would have had Milo with you when it happened."

My gaze moved to the dog, who still lay there with his chin between his paws. Although he looked dejected, I had a feeling that was more because he'd been denied a scone than because his mistress had just died. "I'm pretty sure he would have been," I said. "Unless it was one of the times I let him out to roam around the backyard."

"And you didn't notice any change in his demeanor, anything to show he might have felt it when Darla passed away?"

I paused for a moment as I did my best to recall all the interactions I'd had with Milo after his mistress dropped him off at my house. As far as I could tell, there hadn't been any instances where he seemed particularly upset or had even experienced a moment of pain, something you might have expected to happen when the bond between the two of them was severed forever. If anything, he'd seemed much perkier after Darla had left to go back to Chicago, as though being around her was a sort of weight he'd had to carry, and once she'd dropped him off, he was free to be his usual happy self.

"Nothing like that," I said. "It's like he wasn't connected to her at all."

Grace stared back at me, surprise clear on her plump features. "That doesn't make sense," she said. "The bond between a familiar and their witch is one of the strongest connections in the world."

So I'd been told, and yet everything I'd seen—and everything Stella had told me about Darla's interactions with Milo—seemed to indicate pretty much the exact opposite.

"Theirs wasn't," I said, and glanced over at the dog. He appeared to have dozed off, as if he could tell nothing Grace and I might have to discuss would end up affecting him in any way. "I mean, look at him. Does he look like a familiar who's just lost his mistress?"

Grace pursed her mouth, although she didn't bother to reply. It was painfully obvious to both of us that, according to every bit of witchy wisdom we knew on the subject of familiars, Milo shouldn't have been alive at all, let alone comfortably snoozing on Grace Bowersby's well-worn Persian rug.

As I stared at the dog, though, and watched the gentle rise and fall off his sides as he breathed deeply and calmly, a sudden thought struck me.

"What if he's alive precisely because he and Darla *didn't* have a close bond?"

Grace's light blue eyes flared with surprise, but then she nodded as the import of my question apparently began to sink in. "You might be on to something there, Charity," she said. "I'm still not sure how he could have remained her familiar all those years without that kind of connection, but since it obviously wasn't there, then maybe that was what protected him when she passed away. Without that soul bond, he really wouldn't have been much more than a pet."

Poor Milo. He was a sweetie, and deserved much better than the bum hand fate had apparently dealt him.

Then again, it was still much better than what the universe had decided to deal Darla Fitzgerald.

"Something else is odd, though," Grace went on. "Milo had to have been with Darla for decades, and yet he still looks like a dog in the prime of his life. How could he have kept from aging if their bond wasn't really that close?"

That was a very good question. Unfortunately, I didn't have anything remotely resembling an answer. I lifted my shoulders and said, "Maybe they had just enough of a connection to keep him young, but now that Darla is gone, he'll start to age like a regular dog."

Grace reached up to push away one of the

wispy curls that was perpetually escaping the bun at the back of her neck. "I suppose that's possible. But what's to become of him now?"

"He's staying with me," I replied at once. Fobbing Milo off on someone else wasn't an option. And if Darla's relatives tried to claim him, well, I'd do my best to argue that I was the person best-suited to keep their daughter's former familiar. Possession was nine-tenths of the law, after all. "He's a very good dog."

"Until someone leaves a cat with you to be taken care of," Grace said darkly.

"Well, I'll deal with that problem when and if it happens," I said. "For now, I think the most important thing is for Milo to be in a place where he feels stable and cared for. I can already tell that he loves the yard, so having him around won't be a problem at all."

As I spoke, though, I wondered if I might be acting a little too blithe about the situation. After all, while I'd gotten Sage to cover for me today, I would have to go back to work at the shop sooner rather than later. Would Milo be all right with me leaving him home alone for large chunks of the day?

Then again, I could always bring him with me to the store. I wouldn't be the only shop owner in Salem's historic district who had a pet roaming around, although most of those other mascots were cats. Then again, Milo seemed to be very well-behaved. I could set up a bed for him in the break room and slip out to take him for a walk whenever business was slow. It would be fine.

I hoped.

"Well, that does sound like the perfect situation for him," Grace observed. "And lord knows, the poor thing would probably be much happier staying with someone who actually wants him around."

Poor thing, indeed. I knew it was generally considered a bad idea to speak ill of the dead, but I couldn't quite contain my inner fury at Darla Fitzgerald for being so cavalier about her familiar, who'd only wanted to be there to help her and make her happy. As far as I was concerned—harsh as such a judgment might be—she'd gotten exactly what she deserved.

"I do want him around," I said firmly.

"Of course you do," Grace replied, and leaned over to pat my arm. "I think it's wonderful the way you've stepped up for Milo. And of course I'll keep looking through my records to see if anything like this has ever happened before."

I thanked her, and ate the few remaining bites of my scone. Even though I could have sworn Milo was dead asleep, he seemed to know the instant Grace and I were done with our chat, because he got to his feet and waited for me to clip on his leash

so I could lead him out to my car. It was an old
Land Rover Discovery I'd bought a while back
because I thought it would be useful for trans-
porting my various animal charges, and since the
leather upholstery was already scratched in a
million places, I definitely didn't have to worry
about whether my new companion might leave his
own marks on the seat.

He jumped in and sat up, tongue out, eyes
bright. On the drive over to Grace's house, he'd
been just as animated, wanting to stick his nose out
the window so he could smell the fresh breeze, tail
wagging with soft little whispery sounds against
the leather as it moved back and forth. In fact, he'd
been so excited about getting to ride on the
passenger seat that I had to wonder if Darla had
ever allowed him in her own vehicle.

Probably not; she'd definitely seemed like the
sort of person who'd want her car to be as immacu-
late as her person, and getting a bunch of long
golden hairs all over the interior of her BMW or
Mercedes or whatever it was that she'd driven probably wasn't her idea of a good time.

I had no such concerns, however, and it made
me happy to see Milo sitting over there, long ears
flapping as I picked up speed. Not too much, of
course—we were driving through residential neigh-
borhoods with speed limits of no more than thirty
miles an hour—but apparently it was enough to

make the dog think we were absolutely zooming along.

After we got home and I'd parked the Discovery in my detached one-car garage, we went inside the house. Milo immediately headed over to the water bowl and helped himself to a long drink, while I sent Sage a quick text.

> Sorry I couldn't make it in today.
> So much is going on! I'll tell you
> all about it tomorrow.

She responded almost immediately, letting me know the store still wasn't too busy.

> Glad to help! Dying to hear
> what's going on.

I couldn't help wincing at her choice of words, but to be fair, my assistant couldn't have had any idea about what had happened to Darla Fitzgerald. Word would get around soon enough, in the peculiar grapevine the witch world seemed to share, unless Detective Adams and his cohorts at the Chicago P.D. had decided they needed to keep things under wraps for now.

Hard to say. I wasn't about to call him back, although I wondered whether I should call Stella to let her know what had happened to Darla. After hemming and hawing for a moment, I decided I should stay quiet on the subject. The detective hadn't told me not to talk about Darla's death, but maybe that was because he had no reason to think I'd go spreading the story around. He couldn't know that she and I were both witches, that we were part of an underground group of magic-workers that spanned the globe.

There was no reason for him to find out, either. The crime team probably would have searched her apartment, looking for clues, but I doubted she would keep anything there that would reveal her identity as a witch. Any work she did on the Witch Olympics would be stored off-site somewhere in a location that was enchanted so no one who wasn't also a witch would even be able to locate it, and even if the police had found a few tricks of the trade during their inspection of her apartment—wands or crystals, maybe even a grimoire—they would've thought she was someone who dabbled in witchcraft and paganism and nothing more. Thousands...if not millions...of mundies played with those sorts of things, too, but because they hadn't been born with magic in their veins, none of it would do them any good.

Finished drinking, Milo went over to the kitchen door and let out a low whine. Clearly, he needed to go out to the yard to take care of business.

"You're sure you want to just go in the garden?" I asked him, feeling a little guilty that I hadn't been paying closer attention to his needs. "Wouldn't you rather go for a walk?"

He paused to consider my question, then scratched the back door again. Clearly, my yard was enough of a novelty that he preferred to go out there, even if a walk might have given him the chance to get better acquainted with the neighborhood.

Well, even though he still couldn't speak, he obviously could tell that I planned to keep him, which meant there would be plenty of opportunities in the future for him to go exploring. I opened the kitchen door and said, "Not too long. It's almost time for your dinner."

Or at least, what I assumed was his dinnertime, since we were coming up on six o'clock. Darla hadn't said much about his feeding schedule, probably assuming I'd do it at normal hours. True, he had to still be on Chicago time, and therefore to him it was now only a little before four, but I wanted to get a routine established here early on.

Thinking about Milo's dinner made me wonder what I should do for my own evening meal. There was still some kung pao chicken and fried rice left over from the takeout I'd gotten the day before, and reheating it seemed to be the simplest thing to do. To be honest, I wasn't much for cooking, despite the way I brewed potions on an almost daily basis. Meal prep always seemed like a lot of work, especially when it was just me and even making a batch of chili in my crockpot meant I'd be eating the same thing for a week.

And considering how crazy my day had been, the mere thought of having to gather even a few simple ingredients to whip up something from scratch made me want to break out in hives.

I got out the plastic bag of food Darla had brought for Milo and poured it into his bowl. Even though the woman hadn't exactly made a favorable impression on me...to say the least...I still experienced a pang as I rezipped the baggie. When she'd packed this food for her familiar, she could have had no idea this would be her last day on earth.

A blink, and I told myself that yes, the whole thing was absolutely terrible, but I needed to be present for Milo. True, he didn't seem too upset about his mistress's death, although that could have been because the truth of his situation really hadn't sunk in yet, and he still viewed his stay here with me as a fun break in his routine and not something that had turned out to be permanent.

He'd been out in the yard for quite a while, though. At lunch, as soon as I'd put out his food for him, he'd come running.

I went to the doorway and called out, "Milo! Dinner!"

No answering bark, no golden-brown flash of fur as he hurried toward the kitchen door. I frowned a little, even as I told myself he'd probably found a particularly interesting smell and just wasn't paying any attention.

Still....

I stepped outside. The warmth of the day lingered in the air, although a freshening of the breeze that came off the ocean told me it would probably be cool enough tonight that I'd need to close at least some of the windows.

"Milo!"

Still nothing. Even though it was a mild evening, with the kind of weather that normally would have sent me to sit outside with a glass of white wine and enjoy these all-too-brief late spring days, a shiver went down my spine. I couldn't help thinking of Darla Fitzgerald, found dead in her condo only a few hours earlier.

"Milo?"

This time I sounded hesitant to even myself, as if I knew deep inside there had to be a terrible reason why the dog wasn't responding to my calls.

I went through the herb garden, oblivious to its usually comforting blend of friendly smells, and over to the trees that separated my property from my neighbors to the west, the stand of eastern pine and oak and elm that Milo had found so fascinating.

My breath caught. Lying at the base of a stately oak as old as the house was a bundle of golden fur.

Oh, no—

I ran forward and knelt next to the dog in the fresh spring grass. A stab of relief went through me as I saw that his chest still rose and fell...relief that disappeared as soon as I noticed the awful bloody marks around his throat, the blood that matted his paws.

A wild animal attack? I didn't think that was very likely. Sure, there were black bears in the woods around here and the odd coyote and bobcat sighting, but none of those animals ventured this far inside Salem's town borders.

Not that it mattered. The important thing was to take care of Milo.

I needed to call the vet, but my phone was in my purse inside the kitchen, yards away.

Well, sometimes being a witch came in very handy.

Something as simple as this didn't even require a spell. No, I visualized the phone in my hand, snapped my fingers, and it dropped instantly into my palm.

Noah Jenkins' number was already stored in my contacts, so I didn't have to waste any time looking him up on Google. Except it was now after six, and all I got was the clinic's answering machine.

But....

"If this is an emergency, please call 617-555-3763."

Thank God.

The numbers stuck to my brain like glue, so I didn't have to worry about forgetting them as I entered each one. Was this Noah's personal cell, or just some kind of service he used to intercept after-hours calls?

Then his voice, smooth and unruffled, just like the other times I'd brought an ailing animal to him at the clinic. "Noah Jenkins."

"It's Charity Hughes," I said, not bothering with a greeting or anything else that might waste precious minutes. "The dog I've been watching was attacked by some kind of animal and is bleeding pretty badly. Can you come over?"

"Of course," he replied. "Is the dog stable?"

I had absolutely no idea. Milo was watching me, his chest rising and falling in heavy pants, which told me he was still alive. How long he'd remain that way was anyone's guess.

"I—I don't know."

"It's okay," he said. "I'm coming right over. Just do your best to put pressure on the wounds until I get there. Can you tell me your address again?"

"I'm at 866 Winter Island Drive," I replied, realizing that of course he wouldn't know where I lived, since I'd always come into the clinic before this. The information was probably in my paperwork somewhere, but he had an office assistant to handle that kind of thing and probably hadn't even looked at it.

"I'm less than five minutes away. Just hang on."

He ended the call there, and I dropped my phone into the grass, knowing I'd need both hands for what I had to do next. As far as I could tell, the wounds on Milo's throat were the worst and the ones that required immediate attention.

My black sleeveless dress was long, coming down to almost my ankles. I reached over and tore a wide strip off the bottom, then wadded up the cotton cloth and pressed it against the dog's neck. He whimpered slightly at my touch but didn't try to move away, telling me he knew I was trying to help.

I sat next to Milo in the grass, holding the torn fabric on his throat, and prayed he'd hold on long enough for Noah to get here.

Chapter 6

Bleeding Heart

I KNEW NOAH JENKINS DIDN'T RIDE A broom, but he got to my house so quickly that it felt as though he must have flown...or at least broken several speeding laws on his way over here.

He got down in the grass next to me, saying, "It's okay, Charity. Let me take a look."

With some reluctance, I let go of the blood-stained strip of cloth I'd been holding against Milo's throat. It wasn't that I didn't trust Noah to take good care of the dog, but more that it seemed as if my pressure on the dog's neck had been the only thing keeping him alive, and if I stopped staunching the wounds, what would happen next?

Of course, I should have known Noah had a plan for that. He was already holding gauze bandages and a bottle of iodine, and was ready to dive in just as soon as I dropped the torn fabric to the ground. Milo whimpered again, but there was almost a note of relief in his voice, as if he knew he was in good hands now.

Noah quickly taped down the gauze, then told me, "Okay, that's holding the bleeding enough for me to get him inside. Will he let me pick him up?"

I glanced at Milo, and the dog moved his head almost imperceptibly.

"Yes," I said, and managed a wan smile. "I think he trusts you."

Noah didn't smile back, only reached over so he could pick up the wounded animal and get to his feet. He accomplished the maneuver with a lot more grace than I would have, but then, the vet had a good five or six inches on me and obviously worked out in his spare time, so handling a twenty-five-pound dog wasn't such a big deal.

Immediately, he headed for the open door to the kitchen. Once we were inside, he glanced over at the kitchen table and asked, "Is it okay if I set him down there?"

"Sure," I replied, even as I darted ahead so I could get my purse out of harm's way and drop it to the floor. "Is there anything else you need?"

"Clean cloths and hot water," Noah said, and now smiled a little, those amazing blue eyes of his looking as though they were bright enough to light up an operating theater. "Sounds like I'm delivering a baby, but it'll help get him cleaned up."

Hot water was no problem. I hurried over to the stove and turned on the gas under my teakettle, which I'd filled earlier, and then got out another pan and set it below the tap while I grabbed as many clean dish towels from one of the drawers as I could hold in one hand.

"Is that enough?" I asked anxiously.

"It'll do for now." Noah's tone was almost absent, and I could tell all his focus was on the dog he'd gently laid on top of the kitchen table. The cloth that covered the table was already blotched with blood, but I didn't care. I was just glad Milo was lying on something other than bare wood.

Noah had brought his medical kit with him, and reached in to pull out a pair of scissors so he could trim away some of the bloodstained fur that concealed the true nature of Milo's injuries. With them now laid bare, I could see the long jagged edges of the worst of the wounds, and wondered how in the world he'd ever managed to survive the assault.

"What would do something like that?" I whispered.

Without looking up from his work, Noah replied, "I think you're right that it was some kind of wild animal attack, but I didn't think we had anything big enough around here to cause these kinds of injuries."

"We don't," I said, reminding myself that the

vet had moved here from Boston barely a year ago, and therefore didn't have the same local area knowledge as us natives. "Or at least, there are bears in Massachusetts, but I've never heard of them making it this far east. A coyote couldn't have done this, could it?"

Noah shook his head, although he kept his eyes on Milo as he replied, "They rarely attack a dog this size. Cats...that's a different story."

The kettle began to whistle, and I went over to shut it off. "What do you want me to do with the hot water?"

"Soak some of these towels in it," Noah instructed me. "I want to get him cleaned up as best I can." He paused there before adding, "The good news is, the wounds on his throat are the worst of it. They're the only thing that needs stitching. It looks like the blood on his paws is from him fighting back."

Good for Milo. I sincerely hoped he'd given as good as he got.

As I poured some of the boiling water over a tea towel, Noah went on, "The wounds are strange. If we were farther out west, I'd say maybe it was a big cat that went after him, a mountain lion or something. But we don't have any of those around here, do we?"

I shook my head. "No. Just bobcats, but Milo's too big to be easy prey for one of them."

And he wasn't easy prey, I thought. *He fought back.*

A faint line appeared between Noah's brows as he frowned, but he never stopped working, dabbing at the biggest wound with more iodine. Through all this, Milo didn't move and didn't even utter a sound, as though he knew the best thing to do was lie still and allow the vet to do his work.

"A bear would've killed him outright," Noah added. "But whatever it was, it sure looks to me like your dog fought him off. He's a brave guy."

"Yes, he is," I said, then handed Noah the tea towel I'd just blanched so he could use it to wipe away more of the blood. I hesitated, wondering whether I should say anything else. But then, the vet would find out soon enough that Milo had become a permanent part of my household. "He's having an awfully rough day. I just found out that his owner was killed, so it looks as though he's going to be staying with me unless one of her relatives wants to take him."

Something I doubted would happen. If anyone in Darla Fitzgerald's family had cared about Milo's well-being, then I had to believe they would have stepped in and done something about the way she treated him.

Although Noah had been intent on his work, at my words he paused and sent me a startled glance. "That is rough," he said. "I'm sorry."

"I didn't know her well," I replied. "But yes, it was kind of a shock. And it seemed as though Milo was really liking it here, and I thought he should be able to settle in okay...and then this happened."

Noah set aside the cloth and got out a suture kit from his bags. "Well, he seems like a tough dog. It'll be an adjustment for him, sure, but he'll be in good hands here with you."

Luckily, Noah bent over to start stitching up Milo's wounds right then, so he missed the surprised flush that touched my cheeks at his words of praise. Maybe the vet would have said much the same thing to anyone, and yet I couldn't help feeling encouraged, had to believe he'd noticed how much I loved animals.

Wouldn't that make us compatible?

I told myself I shouldn't be thinking about that kind of thing, not with Milo lying there covered in both his own blood and the blood of his unknown attacker, but my brain didn't quite want to let it alone. After all, a shared love of animals seemed like a pretty good reason for two people to get together.

"Thank you," I murmured, but Noah was so intent on his work, I didn't know for sure whether he even heard me or not.

Which was fine. The important thing right now was to make sure Milo survived the attack and went on to have a long and healthy life. How long that life would be, I honestly didn't know for sure, since we were definitely in uncharted territory here. I'd never heard of a familiar surviving his mistress's death, and neither had Grace. Maybe she'd find some precedent for such a thing in the messy stack of files she called her archives and maybe she wouldn't, but either way, I planned to love Milo for as long as I had him with me.

Five minutes or so went by, and then another five. I tried to keep myself from glancing at the little antique clock that hung on the wall above the kitchen window, but its ticking was so loud, it was impossible to ignore the passing of time. From what I could tell, though, Noah had attended to the worst of Milo's wounds first before going on to the others. Three of them required stitches, but the rest he just covered with gauze and taped down after trimming away some of the fur that surrounded them.

At last, though, Noah turned away from the dog and gave me a weary smile. "That just about does it," he said. "The wounds were clean enough, so I don't think we need to worry about infection. I'm going to leave you some antibiotics, though, just to be safe, and some drops for the pain. You'll need to give him those three times a day for the first couple of days, and then see how he does after that."

"Thank you so much," I said, hoping he could hear the gratitude in my voice. "I don't know what

I would have done if you hadn't picked up the phone."

"Well, if it's too late in the day, I forward those calls to the twenty-four-hour clinic on the other side of town," Noah told me. "But otherwise, I try to be here for my clients." He reached over and patted Milo on the head, and the dog gave him a lick of his hand before his eyelids drooped and he lay back against the table.

Poor thing.

"Is it safe to move him?" I asked. "He'd be a lot more comfortable in his bed than up on that table."

Noah nodded. "It'll be okay. Better let me do it, though."

He bent over so he could gather up the limp dog, and I showed him where Milo's bed had been set down in the living room next to the fireplace. With him in such a state, he might have been better off upstairs in my bedroom, but I figured I'd sleep on the couch tonight to keep him company and then see how he was doing the next day before I made him climb all those steps or risked jostling his wounds by carrying him myself.

After Noah had set the dog gently in his bed, he straightened up and looked at me. A little thrill went down my spine, even though there was absolutely nothing in his gaze except professional courtesy.

"Keep him from moving around as much as you can," he said. "It looks like he's going to pull through just fine, but I don't want him over-extending himself and messing with those stitches. And I'll try to drop by tomorrow and check to see how he's doing."

"Thank you," I said again, then added before I could lose my nerve, "It's dinnertime—do you want me to order something in? I hate to think of you going home and having to fix something after everything you've just done for us."

Maybe I spied just the slightest bit of hesitation. But then Noah smiled and asked, "Does anyone deliver all the way out here?"

"Gino's does," I said, naming the pizza place that had been a fixture in my life ever since I was old enough to eat solid food. "As long as you're up for pizza, of course."

"Pizza sounds great," Noah replied.

With that settled—and after we both decided on the works for our toppings—I called in the order. It would take about twenty minutes, but that gave me a chance to set the dining room table, and ask Noah...all the while hoping I didn't sound too timid...if he'd like a beer or a glass of wine with his pizza.

I'd halfway expected him to demur, but apparently Noah had decided he'd earned a drink after performing that emergency surgery.

"Some wine would be great," he said, and I found myself relaxing. If he wasn't interested in me at all, he would have said no, right?

Maybe, or maybe not. I decided it didn't really matter, that the important thing was that he was going to stay for pizza and some chianti.

I poured a glass for each of us—not too full, since he'd have to drive home after this—and said, "I really do appreciate you coming here to help Milo. I don't know what I would have done if—"

The words broke off there, and I made myself stop. It was easy to imagine the worst possible outcome, but that hadn't happened. No, Noah Jenkins had come to the rescue, and now Milo was sleeping peacefully in his bed. Whether the painkillers he'd been given would be enough to keep him knocked out once the house smelled of pepperoni and sausage was a conundrum I'd have to face in the very near future, but for the moment, it was enough to know the dog was going to make it.

As to what had attacked him, well, I'd have to ask about that once we were safely alone and Milo was rested enough to try communicating with me. I could only imagine Noah's reaction if he saw me questioning a dog the way I might interrogate the eyewitness to a crime.

"It's okay," Noah said quietly. "The important thing is that I got your call, and my house isn't too far away. I was able to get here before he lost too much blood. Otherwise, I probably would have had to move him to the clinic so he could be watched 'round the clock."

Right—the clinic itself wasn't open twenty-four/seven, but besides his office assistant, Noah had several vet techs who provided coverage to keep an eye on the animals that needed to stay there overnight following surgery.

"I'm glad Milo's able to stay here," I said. "He's already had enough shocks today without having to sleep in a strange place."

Noah looked as though he was about to reply, but the doorbell rang then, and I hurried over to open the door and hand some money to the pizza delivery guy. He didn't look familiar, telling me he was probably a college student looking to make some extra cash during summer break.

The doorbell hadn't roused Milo, but as soon as I set the pizza box on the dining room table and popped the top, he cracked an eyelid and looked around, albeit blearily.

Noah went to the dog and petted him on the head, telling him, "You need to stay put, boy. But if you're good and stay in your bed, maybe Charity will give you a piece of pepperoni."

That offer made me raise an eyebrow. "I thought all you vets frown on giving dogs table scraps."

"It's not the best thing in the world for them," Noah replied, looking unperturbed. "In this case, though, I think he's earned it."

Apparently Milo was ready to take his savior at his word, because he stayed quiet in his bed while the two of us sat down at the dining room table and served ourselves some pizza. Making a toast seemed kind of silly, considering the circumstances, so I just sipped some chianti before digging into my slice of loaded pizza.

Yes, this was way better than reheating kung pao chicken and eating it alone.

Noah also seemed ready for some serious sustenance, since he consumed several bites of his slice before he set it down on his plate and sent me a very direct look. "I thought you mostly fostered," he said, "but earlier you said you knew Milo's owner."

Oh, damn. I'd been so shaken by what had happened to the dog that I hadn't expended much energy on watching my words. "Well, she dropped him off," I said carefully. "I didn't really *know* her. In this particular case, she brought him to me because she knew I fostered a lot of animals and she was considering rehoming him."

"'Rehoming him'?" Noah repeated, looking startled. "But he seems like such a good dog."

"He is," I said. Maybe the rest of what I'd been saying was pure fiction...necessary fiction, I reminded myself, even though I really disliked the idea of lying to Noah Jenkins...but that particular observation was nothing more than the truth. "His owner didn't give me a lot of details. I got the impression that she worked long hours and lived in a condo, and it's not the best environment for a dog who needs attention and room to roam."

Luckily, this story must have sounded plausible to Noah, because he didn't try to pick any holes in it and only nodded, looking a little sad. I had to believe he'd seen situations like this all too many times, where people took animals into their homes without understanding what such a commitment would actually require of them.

"Her loss," he said. "I'm glad he's going to be with someone who has the resources to care for him."

I didn't know if Noah had intended that comment as a form of praise or not, but I thought I'd take it. And unlike Grace, he hadn't asked me whether bringing a dog into my home on a full-time basis would interfere with all the other animals I might foster. Maybe he didn't think it was any of his business, or maybe he'd just decided that I knew what I was doing and it wasn't his place to comment.

Either way, we had a pleasant dinner, with him talking about Salem and asking me for advice on local restaurants and such, while I gave him my insights as a life-long resident and did my best not to stare too hard at him, at the strong, friendly features and clear blue eyes, or the long, deft fingers as they wrapped themselves around a slice of pizza. Oddly, though, it was easier to be with him like this across a dining room table than it was standing a few feet away at the clinic while he discussed what was going on with my latest foster. Possibly, it was simply that this felt like a couple of friends sitting and chatting, and therefore was a much more relaxed situation.

Whatever the reason, that hour or so passed easily enough, and after we were done with our pizza, we both went over to Milo with our offerings, a small slice of pepperoni from me and a little chunk of sausage from Noah. The dog opened an eye just long enough to consume both morsels, then fell asleep again almost immediately.

"That's the best thing for him," Noah said, after he'd retrieved his black doctor's bag and walked with me to the front door. "Lots and lots of rest."

I nodded. "I'm going to sleep down here on the couch tonight, just so I can keep watch."

Instead of telling me I didn't need to go to such extreme lengths, Noah only looked pleased. "That's a good idea. And if he takes a turn for the worse— if he spikes a fever or has a seizure—call me right away."

"He could have a seizure?" I asked, alarmed.

"It's not very likely," Noah said at once. "But I just wanted to warn you. Anyway, call me and I'll come over."

"Even if it's two in the morning?"

"Even then," he reassured me, his steady gaze telling me he was utterly sincere about the offer.

I didn't think that would happen, but I still thanked him, then waited at the front door as he walked down the porch steps and over to the white pickup truck parked at the curb. It wasn't until he'd pulled away that I shut the door and allowed myself to release a breath.

It wasn't exactly the first date I'd pictured in my wistful daydreams, but I'd still had dinner with Noah Jenkins.

I figured I'd take it.

Chapter 7

Shadow Dance

Surprisingly, I slept better on the couch than I'd expected to. Quite possibly, it was only because I'd had such an exhausting day that my body wouldn't allow me to not get its minimum of seven hours of sleep, but either way, I conked out a lot harder than I'd expected to. Once in the middle of the night, I woke up, worried about Milo, but a pause to glance over at him—I'd left one lamp on with the dimmer turned down almost as low as it could go—told me he was sleeping soundly, chest rising and falling, feet and tail twitching every once in a while, as though he was chasing rabbits in his dreams.

Soon, I promised him. Not that I would actually let him catch a rabbit, but scaring a few of those critters away from my garden could only be a good thing. I'd placed warding spells around the flower and herb beds, but either my enchantments weren't entirely up to snuff or rabbits were much more determined creatures than I gave them credit for, because they kept coming back no matter what I did.

I slept like the dead the rest of the night, and when I woke up a little past seven, it was to see Milo watching me, although he hadn't tried to climb out of his bed.

"Good morning," I told him, then pushed myself up from the couch so I could go over and pet him on the head. His eyes were bright and he didn't seem feverish at all, which cheered me up that much more. Noah had done a great job of patching him up, and now it was on me to make sure my new canine companion healed as quickly as possible. "Do you think you can go out?"

Milo's tail wagged, but a little hesitantly, as if he wanted to tell me he definitely needed to go in the backyard but wasn't sure whether he could make it on his own.

That was why I carefully scooped him up and carried him out back, then set him down on the nearest patch of grass. Because I thought it was rude to stare while he was doing his business, I turned partly away, just enough so it wouldn't look as though I was watching but where I could still keep him in my peripheral vision in case his attacker from the day before decided to reappear.

All was still and quiet that morning, though, except for the birds chirping cheerfully in the trees, and the beginnings of a fresh sea breeze that rustled through the bright green leaves on the oaks and elms and brought with it the wild, salty scent of the ocean. It was hard to believe that any kind of violence could have occurred in such a peaceful place, but clearly, we needed to remain on our guard.

Business attended to, Milo walked slowly over to the back steps. I hovered a few feet behind, ready to dive in and scoop him up if necessary, but it appeared as though he wanted to prove to himself that he could manage the stairs on his own. He climbed up one laborious step at a time and looked positively triumphant when he reached the stoop.

The two of us went inside, where I gave him his breakfast and then started boiling water for that morning's tea. Sometimes I drank coffee, but the fresh day seemed to call for a hot cup of oolong and a muffin.

As much as I wanted to relax and enjoy myself, I knew I needed to text Sage and let her know I wouldn't be able to make it in today, either. Although Milo seemed to be on the road to recovery, I thought it was best to stay home with him and make sure he didn't get into any trouble.

I'm so sorry about this, but I'm
going to have to skip today, too.
I'll make it up to you, promise!

No worries. You do what you
need to. It probably won't get
crazy until next weekend,
anyway.

Next weekend, which was Memorial Day and the unofficial start of summer. Foot traffic on historic Essex Street had been picking up for the past couple of weeks, but once summer was truly upon us, things wouldn't really start to slow down until after Halloween, which was always the event of the year in Salem. I added,

I'll be in way before then.

At least, I hoped so. Once Milo was truly on the mend, then I'd probably bring him to work with me. Right now, though, he needed some peace and quiet.

"I've gotta shower, kiddo," I told him. "Think you can hold down the fort here for a while?"

He nodded, looking solemn, although I went ahead and closed and locked the back door, and made sure all the windows on the ground floor were shut and locked tight as well. Normally, I wouldn't take those kinds of precautions, because my neighborhood was a safe one and I liked to have fresh air flowing through my house whenever the weather permitted.

Right now, though, since I had no idea what we were up against and what had attacked Milo in the garden the day before, it seemed best to exercise caution. I also murmured a quick spell to alert me if anything bigger than a cat crossed over my property line, and figured I'd done my due diligence.

All the same, I made the shower a quick one, not bothering to wash my hair because I'd already done so the day before. My wavy-on-the-verge-of-curly hair only needed a few squirts from the spray bottle of water I kept under the bathroom sink to make it look mostly presentable, and I guessed that should be enough. After all, I wasn't going in to work today, so it wasn't as though I needed to impress anybody.

Well, unless Noah Jenkins decided he really did need to stop by and check on Milo.

I might as well have cast a summoning spell right then, because just thinking of the handsome vet was enough to make my cell phone ring from the spot where I'd left it on the nightstand before I got in the shower. Sure enough, the number displayed on the home screen was Noah's.

"Just wanted to check on my patient," he said. Somewhere in the background behind him, I could hear barking dogs and what sounded like two women talking, and I guessed he was already at the clinic.

"He's fine," I replied. "He slept all night, and he ate all his breakfast. He's moving a little slowly, but it already looks as though he's well on his way to healing up."

"That's great news. Do you mind if I swing by on my way home today so I can take a look at him myself?"

Did I mind? There was a question. Of course I didn't. As far as I was concerned, Noah could drop in any time he liked.

"That's fine," I said, hoping I sounded nonchalant. "I'm going to stay home today to keep an eye on him, but I'm sure he'll do fine."

"Probably a good idea. You don't want him to get stressed by being left alone in the house."

No, I didn't. I made a noncommittal sound, and Noah continued.

"Don't forget to give him his medication three times a day until it runs out."

"I won't," I promised, even though it had already slipped my mind that morning, since I'd been more focused on feeding him and getting him outside to go potty. True, I probably would have remembered the dog's medication once I opened the refrigerator door and saw it sitting in there, but I mentally thanked Noah for the reminder.

"Then I should be by around five-thirty, maybe

a little afterward," he told me. "It depends on whether my last appointment of the day runs long."

I assured him it wouldn't be a problem, and we ended the call there. Then I headed downstairs, where I found Milo back in his bed, chin on his bandaged paws. He looked so glum that I kneeled down and scratched him behind the ears, and said, "It's okay, Milo. Before you know it, you'll be back running around the yard."

"I'm not sure I want to go out there by myself," the dog responded, and I stared at him, flabbergasted.

Had Milo just *talked* to me?

Under ordinary circumstances, I wouldn't have been so shocked. After all, that was my talent—talking to other people's familiars.

But he hadn't spoken a word since he got here, thanks to that nasty little spell Darla Fitzgerald had cast on him.

"Did you...?" I began, then stopped.

"Yes, I just talked," Milo replied. Like a lot of dogs, he had a sort of gravelly voice, not really a growl because it sounded too friendly, but with enough grit running along the bottom that it didn't sound exactly like a human's voice, either.

"But the spell—"

"I know," he said. "I haven't been able to talk for almost two weeks. Then this morning after having my breakfast and getting some fresh air, it just...came back."

About all I could do was shake my head. "Well, I'm glad to hear it. Maybe Darla's spell finally wore off?"

"That must be it," Milo replied. "I sort of thought the enchantment would go away as soon as she died, but it looks like it was strong enough that it lingered for a while after she was gone."

He sounded completely matter-of-fact when he mentioned his former mistress, telling me that my guess about him not being too upset regarding the situation had been right. Still, I couldn't help venturing, "Do you...do you want to talk about it?"

"About what?" Milo said. "You mean Darla?"

I nodded.

His tail thumped against the side of his bed, but it seemed more like a dog's version of a shrug than an indication that he was particularly happy. "I'm sorry she went before her time, but she wasn't a very good mistress. She always acted completely put upon to have a dog around."

Again, that was the impression I'd gotten. "So...you're not sad?"

Milo scrunched his nose. "Not sad for me. Sad for her, I suppose."

A down-to-earth way to look at the situation, I thought. While animals' personalities varied a lot from one to the other, they tended to be much more practical than humans. So, while Milo could acknowledge it wasn't a good thing to be snuffed out in the prime of life, he also wasn't going to dance around the fact that Darla hadn't treated him very well, and he was more than glad to be with someone else now.

"How do you feel?" I asked, figuring it was probably a good idea to change the subject...for now, anyway. With Milo talking again, I really needed to pick his brain about what Darla had been up to in the weeks before she died and why she'd thought it was a good idea to try silencing her familiar, but I wanted to check in with his health situation before I did anything else. And I also thought it better to not question him too closely about the attack right now, not when he was still feeling weak and shaky. It definitely seemed as though whatever had attacked him had come and gone, and wasn't posing a current threat to the neighborhood.

"I'm all right," Milo said in response to my question, then paused as though to take a quick assessment of his current physical condition. "I hurt, but it's a bearable kind of hurt."

Reminding me again that he needed this morning's dose of painkillers. "I've got something for that," I told him. "Let me get it from the fridge."

I hurried into the kitchen and retrieved the

little bottle of medicine from the refrigerator, then carefully filled up the dropper. Back in the living room, I instructed Milo to open his mouth so I could administer the dose, which he did in a resigned sort of way.

"That tastes like yuck," he said, black lips pulling back from his teeth to show his distaste.

"Worse than my potion from yesterday?"

His head tilted as he considered my question. "I suppose so. But that one was yucky, too, just in a different way."

Since I'd also had to taste the potion, I could agree that it wasn't exactly in my top ten when it came to yummy elixirs. "Well," I said lightly, "since you're talking now, I don't have any reason to use the mind-reading potion again. Why don't you sleep a bit, and then we can chat when you're feeling more rested?"

"I'm fine," Milo protested. However, his eyelids drooped as he spoke, giving the lie to his words.

Obviously, the painkillers were already kicking in.

"I have things to do in the kitchen, though," I said. "I'll come check on you when I'm done."

"'Kay," the dog said in a mumble. His head drooped to the cushion of his bed, and a moment later, he was out like a light.

That must be some good stuff, I thought with a grin.

But because Milo was clearly going to be out of it for a while, I headed off to the kitchen as promised.

After all, if I was going to have an unexpected day off work, I might as well make the best of it.

Milo slept nearly until noon. I'd just finished bottling a batch of my famous spring tonic—a pick-me-up that locals and tourists alike swore by, and which I claimed was effective because of its cheerful mix of dandelion, rhubarb, and strawberry but was also helped along with a small spell to make it even more potent—when the dog meandered into the kitchen, looking a little bleary but walking much more surely than he had earlier.

"Lunch?" he said hopefully.

"Coming right up."

I scooped some Blue Buffalo for him and reminded myself that I'd need to go to the pet store soon, since he only had enough left to last about a day. Well, now that he was talking again, I felt a little better about leaving him by himself, and by tomorrow, he should be even more improved.

"Sounds like you had a good nap," I remarked as I slid a couple of pieces of leftover pizza into the toaster oven. The microwave would have been faster, but I abhorred limp pizza.

"I did," Milo agreed, then lowered his head into his bowl of food.

Since I knew he'd be incommunicado for the next couple of minutes, I went ahead and poured myself a glass of iced tea, then got out a plate for my pizza.

By the time I was done with these tasks, he'd finished his food and was now sniffing hopefully in the direction of the toaster oven. "That smells really good."

"It does," I agreed. "And maybe I'll give you a piece of pepperoni or sausage if you can tell me something about why Darla cast that silencing spell on you."

Dogs couldn't exactly frown, but judging by the way he wrinkled his nose, he wasn't too happy about my conditions for giving him a treat. "I don't know why she did that," he said. "I always did my best to be quiet around her because she didn't like me to talk."

Not for the first time, I experienced a stir of not-unreasonable dislike for the dead woman. Some animals were more talkative than others, but part of the joy of having a familiar was getting to converse with a being who was just happy to be near you, no matter what. Hearing that Darla had wanted Milo to shut up made me angry all over again.

And that was why I plucked the choicest pieces of pepperoni and sausage from my lunch and placed them in Milo's bowl. "If you don't remember anything, it's fine," I told him. "But you've definitely earned this."

For a moment, he only looked back at me. "I would have told you anyway," he said.

"I know," I replied. "You're a good dog."

His tail wagged in response to the compliment, and although he couldn't exactly perk up his long, floppy ears, everything about him looked much cheerier. "Thanks."

He bent and practically swallowed whole the couple of yummy morsels I'd just placed in his bowl, then sat back on his haunches and licked his chops.

"She'd been acting strange for the past couple of months," he said. "That is, she never talked much to me about what was going on in her life, but she sometimes had people from her company or the Witch Olympics committee over to her condo, and she didn't do anything to hide those meetings from me. Not that she needed to," the dog added, nose wrinkling a bit, "because they were boring and I just went to sleep. But starting in late March or somewhere around there, she started making sure I was around as little as possible. She had my dog walker keep me out for hours at a time—"

"Darla didn't walk you herself?" I broke in, startled by that revelation. I supposed if I'd stopped to think about it, such behavior would have jibed with her general treatment of her familiar, but for her to not even take a half hour or so out of her day to be with her dog....

"Nope," Milo replied. He didn't seem very upset by the situation, however. "To be honest, I liked it. Brittany was nice, and I got to be with at least three or four other dogs every time we went for a walk, so that gave me some time to just hang out, you know?"

I hadn't thought about it from that perspective, but Milo's comments made a lot of sense. Dogs were social creatures, and although they could be perfectly happy on their own if they had an attentive family to give them lots of love, having the chance to be around others of his kind had probably made what sounded to me like a sad existence much more bearable.

"So, you spent a lot of time with Brittany the dog-walker," I said. "And you never were able to figure out exactly why Darla wanted you out of the house so much?"

"Nope," Milo replied. Again, he didn't look particularly upset about any of this, but cockers were good-natured, happy-go-lucky dogs, not the type given to brooding. "There was one thing, though."

"What?" I asked, ears pricking up. To tell the truth, I didn't know why I was so interested in learning about what Darla had been up to, except this all smelled like some kind of mystery to me, and even though I didn't read mystery novels or watch police procedurals or anything like that, I still hated having questions unanswered. My mother would have said that was due to my practical Virgo nature. However, I wasn't sure how much credence I wanted to put into astrology, even though she swore by it. "Did you see something suspicious?"

Milo shook, then gingerly settled himself on the kitchen rug. Although he seemed to be doing much better today, I had to believe he still must hurt all over. In fact, it was just about time to give him his midday dose of medicine, but I wanted to hear what he had to say first in case the painkillers knocked him out again.

"It might have been suspicious," he said. "I don't know for sure. But about a week ago, Brittany was running late picking me up, so Darla said she would take me down to the lobby to meet her. We were standing there when a man came up to Darla and asked her why she was meeting him in the lobby instead of in her condo. She brushed him off, and he seemed annoyed and went away. Then

Brittany showed up with the rest of my walk friends, and we went outside."

This sounded a little odd, but maybe Darla had a boyfriend she was trying to keep away from her familiar. The little I knew of her seemed as though she lived a pretty solitary existence, although I'd be the first to admit there were huge portions of her life I knew absolutely nothing about.

"Had you seen the man before?" I asked, and Milo shook his head, long, furry ears swinging a bit.

"No, but he smelled sort of familiar. But if he met Darla at her apartment sometimes, then I suppose he might have left his scent behind."

I should have realized the dog would be more interested in how the man smelled than what he looked like. And if Milo had picked up his scent before, it seemed to indicate the man had been in the condo at least once, maybe more.

Getting a dog to describe a human was always difficult, but I figured I'd better try.

"Can you tell me what he looked like?"

Milo sent a wistful look at the half-eaten slice of pizza on my plate, and I obligingly plucked off another piece of sausage and handed it to him. After he swallowed the morsel, he said, "He was taller than Darla."

Okay, that was a start. "As tall as Dr. Jenkins?"

"No," Milo replied immediately. "Between you and Dr. Jenkins."

Which meant the stranger could be anywhere between five foot seven and a little over six feet. Taller than Darla, though, who was several inches shorter than me but who carried herself like someone blessed with much more height than that.

"Did he have brown hair, like Dr. Jenkins?"

"No. It was light."

"Like mine?" I asked, and pointed at one of the coppery strands that lay against the shoulder of the black embroidered top I was wearing.

"No. Almost as light as Darla's, but not exactly."

So the stranger was medium height and had dark blond hair. While there were definitely more dark-haired men in the United States than there were blonds, I had to admit that particular piece of information didn't narrow things down very much. And apparently, the man had a habit of meeting Darla at her condo when she knew her familiar wouldn't be around.

On the surface, none of that seemed too suspicious. It was entirely possible she'd been dating someone but wanted to keep things quiet because she didn't want the stranger to meet Milo. There were quite a few witches who had relationships but never got married or settled into a long-term commitment with someone because they couldn't find anyone to share the secrets they needed to hide from the world. And I had to guess it must be even harder when you had a familiar, an animal who was supposed to be a part of every aspect of your life.

If Darla hadn't turned up dead, none of this would have been cause for any closer scrutiny. But because someone had killed her, then that meant I needed to take a closer look at all the people in her life, including the mystery man she'd shooed out of the lobby of her condo building.

That was where I stopped myself. I wasn't a detective or anyone with any kind of experience conducting a murder investigation. This was something that should be left up to the police, even if the crime did involve a member of the witch community.

Except...Milo had been attacked. If we were only dealing with Darla's death, I might have left it alone. But someone or something had come on my property and gone after an innocent dog, and I couldn't let that offense stand without at least trying to figure out who was responsible.

"Well, this is very helpful, Milo," I said, guessing that the dog didn't have much more to offer on the subject of the fair-haired stranger who'd been at Darla's building a week earlier. "But now I think it's time to give you your medicine."

He let out a resigned sort of chuff but didn't protest, and meekly swallowed the medication before curling up in his bed so he could sleep off its effects.

As for me, I didn't quite know what to do next, but I did know one thing.

No way in the world was I going to let this go.

Chapter 8

Prints Charming

EVEN THOUGH I'D ALREADY DONE A LITTLE to delve into Darla's past, I thought I'd give it another try, especially since Milo was asleep and I didn't have much to do with myself. True, I could have brewed up more elixirs against the inevitable onslaught of tourists that were sure to invade my shop the following weekend, but I needed to be focused on my work when making tinctures and tonics, and right then I was feeling anything but focused.

Well, on making a batch of brew, anyway.

I went into my office and fetched my laptop, then headed out to the living room so I could work and keep an eye on Milo at the same time. He was already deeply asleep, and once again I had to marvel at the way he seemed so happy and healthy despite the attack, and even though every bit of witch wisdom I possessed regarding familiars told me he shouldn't be alive at all.

But now that we were in the same room together, and anything that tried to attack him again would have to get past me first, I thought it was safe enough to try doing more research on Darla Fitzgerald.

A little more digging located a Facebook account that I thought was hers, something I found kind of puzzling. In general, witches tended to avoid social media, mostly because we always had to work to make sure the general public couldn't detect anything odd about us.

Anyway, even though I guessed it was her account, there wasn't much to find, since it looked as though she had it pretty locked down. She mentioned the PR firm as her place of business, and had her degree from Northwestern listed in her bio, but if she'd made any posts on that account, she must have limited them to friends or maybe friends of friends, because the only thing that was public was a picture of a park somewhere in Chicago, green and friendly.

I stared at my laptop's screen and frowned. There was probably some way to get into her account and see all the posts she wanted to hide from prying eyes, but I was a witch, not a hacker.

Then again....

Witches tended to be jacks—or maybe jills—of

all trades, and could do everything from riding broomsticks to brewing potions. True, we tended to focus on the tasks we were best at, but still, possessing witchy powers meant there was a whole lot of stuff out there we could manage if we just put our minds to it.

Including hacking Facebook...maybe.

I glanced over at Milo, but he was still down for the count and would probably stay that way until he woke up around mid-afternoon and wanted to go out in the backyard. That gave me a few hours.

Time to make a spell.

In magic, intention was everything, but incantations allowed witches to focus those inten- tions and direct them where those concentrated thoughts needed to go. And in this case, that meant Darla's Facebook account.

This kind of task would probably require more caffeine.

I took another look at Milo, but he was still fast asleep. Besides, I was only going a few yards away into the kitchen.

Sure enough, my paranoia was completely unfounded, because absolutely nothing had changed when I returned to the living room. A warm breeze blew at the cheerful blue and green striped curtains at the window, a happy bouquet of daisies and Queen Anne's lace bloomed on the mantel, and Milo had started to snore a bit.

I smiled, then sat back down on the couch and opened my laptop. Darla's picture gazed back at me from her profile page, and I drew in a breath.

Oh, Facebook
Just a look
A peek at her life
To uncover its strife.

Maybe there was the faintest blink as the pixels on the laptop's screen rearranged themselves. And then....

All her posts were displayed on the screen as if they'd been there all along. A lot of funny memes, which seemed out of character for her, and several photos of her with a fair-haired man who also looked as though he was in his early forties. Those pictures had all been taken outside, away from her condo, and featured the two of them smiling at the phone's camera as one of them snapped the selfie.

There were also a number of exchanges between her and the man, whose name appeared to be Dave Michaels. However, when I clicked on the link to take me to his profile, it was mostly blank, only showing his name and his hometown of Saint

Louis, Missouri. All the posts on his wall were of the same pictures I'd seen on Darla's page.

Which meant...what? That he'd only created the profile so he could interact with Darla?

It looked that way to me, although I had to admit I wasn't an expert. I didn't have a Facebook profile or an Instagram account. I wasn't on Twitter or TikTok. My shop had a website, and that was about it when it came to my online footprint.

Who are you, Dave Michaels?

With a name as common as that, I doubted I'd have an easy time tracking him down. Still, I dutifully entered his name and "Saint Louis," and even tried searching on his name and Darla's together, and couldn't find anything useful.

Well, that was annoying.

But maybe I could try an image look-up.

I right-clicked on one of the photos from his profile, then put that in Google. However, the search engine only sent me back to Facebook. As far as I could tell, the man didn't seem to exist, except for his lone social media account.

Double annoying...and mystifying.

Sounded like it was time for another spell, one that would reveal who Dave Michaels really was.

Time to unveil the mystery man
Show me, Facebook, if you can

The man behind the face
Just in case
He's something more than just a fan.

Unlike the enchantment I'd just cast to hack into Darla's Facebook page, however, this one went winging out into the ether...and absolutely nothing happened.

Who was this guy?

I had no idea, and apparently neither the internet...nor my magic...was going to oblige me with the answers I needed. A disgusted breath escaped my lips, and Milo stirred in his bed.

"What're you doing?"

"Trying to find out who Darla's mystery man is," I said. "But I'm getting bupkis."

The dog's head tilted to one side. "What's 'bupkis'?"

"Absolutely nothing," I replied. "But I'm not giving up yet. Do you need to go outside, though?"

At once, Milo got to his feet, his movements a little less labored than they'd been the day before. "Yes, I need to go."

This time, he wanted to walk under his own power, even though every step down from the back stoop looked as though it pained him. Once he was out on the open grass, though, his pace picked up. I lengthened my stride to make sure I was no more than a few feet away from him, although it was hard to believe anything would try to attack him on such a bright, sunny day.

But it had been bright and sunny the day before, too, which meant I couldn't let my guard down for a minute. As I tagged along, I kept scanning the perimeter of the yard, halfway expecting to see a bear drop over the wall, or maybe a coyote come running from the direction of the cove.

None of that happened, of course, even if Milo did get a little closer to the trees than I would have liked. After he was done and I was just about to turn back toward the house, however, something in a muddy patch of earth caught my eye.

A paw print.

Not Milo's, either; I knew enough to be able recognize a dog's footprint right away, as well as that of a domestic cat's or those of the kinds of critters who generally liked to hang around my property—chipmunks, squirrels, rabbits, the odd fox.

This was different, though.

I couldn't linger to inspect it more closely, though, because Milo was surging ahead, obviously ready to go back inside now that he'd been able to stretch his legs a bit. And even though the sight of that lone paw print troubled me, I knew I needed to stay with the dog for now and make sure he got safely inside the house.

Which of course he did. After slurping down some of the water in his bowl, he headed back to bed. As far as I was able to tell, he intended to rest vigorously so he could be back in fighting form sooner rather than later.

Once he was asleep, though—and once I'd added another layer of enchanted protection to my home—I went back outside, this time with some plaster of Paris in hand. I kept all sorts of crafty stuff like that around the house, since I never knew what kind of odd component I might need to seal a spell jar or create a special piece to decorate the house or my shop.

This time, though, I just wanted to get a physical relic of the paw print I'd spied earlier in the garden. We didn't have any rain forecast for the next couple of days, but I didn't see the point in taking any chances and having it possibly get washed away, or maybe overlaid by Milo's own footprints.

No, I wanted to make sure that paw print was preserved for posterity.

I mixed up the plaster on the spot with some water I'd brought along in a measuring cup, then poured it into the print. Since I'd never done anything like this before, I had to hope I was getting it mostly right and wasn't destroying the very piece of evidence I was trying to save.

As I waited for the plaster to set up, I scanned the immediate area, wondering what I would do if the same marauding wild animal decided to pay me a visit. True, I wasn't exactly helpless—at the very least, I could cast a blowback spell to push it into the water and gain myself some time—but since I'd never had to use magic in a high-stress situation before, I honestly had no idea whether I'd be able to keep my wits about me or whether I'd just stand there like the proverbial deer in the headlights.

However, everything remained calm and peaceful. A flock of ducks floated near the rocky beach that was the northern perimeter of my property, and a few more birds flew overhead, but those were the only signs of any wildlife.

I squatted down and pressed my finger against the plaster to see whether it had hardened yet. It still felt faintly moist, telling me I needed to wait a few more minutes. Even though everything seemed quiet enough, I couldn't quite ignore the uneasy feeling at the back of my neck, one that told me I'd left Milo alone way too long.

He's fine, I reassured myself. *If anyone—or anything—tries to get past the warding spells, you'll know right away.*

Which was only the truth, and yet I knew I was all too aware of the seconds and minutes passing by.

At last, though, the plaster felt as if it had hardened enough for me to lift it from the ground. The raised image of a semi-rounded paw with four longish toes showed clearly enough, even though the edges weren't perfect.

A bear?

It didn't look exactly like a bear's paw, though —too round, and with no visible claw marks.

Then again, I was hardly an expert.

Still, now that I had the evidence I needed, I hurried back into the house. To my relief, Milo was still asleep in his bed, snoring faintly.

I resisted the urge to reach down and pat him on the head—after all, I didn't want to wake him up when he needed his rest to heal—and instead went over to my laptop where it still sat on the coffee table. A quick search on Google led me to a paw print identification site, which didn't help me as much as I'd hoped it would. The print I'd pulled from the earth looked somewhere between a bear paw and a tiger paw, but not exactly like either one of them.

Maybe I had really messed up the plaster of Paris cast. That print did look more tiger-ish than something from a bear.

Tigers definitely weren't native to New England, that was for sure. On the other hand, I knew for a fact that they were popular among people who liked to keep exotic pets.

Did anyone around Salem own a tiger?

Not that I was aware of. It was possible anyone who had one as a pet was keeping that information on the down-low, since, even if it wasn't illegal to own a tiger in our state—which I didn't know for sure—then I had to believe they'd still need to have a whole bunch of special permits to keep one.

In which case, I kind of doubted they'd be letting it loose to attack innocent cocker spaniels.

No, this attack had to have been planned...but by whom? Another witch?

I dismissed that idea right away. Some witch familiars could be a little unusual, but those animals were never bigger than a human could handle. I'd never heard of a tiger familiar, or any kind of wild cat as a witch's companion.

And if the person controlling the tiger was just a mundie, why would they have it attack Milo?

Once again, none of this made any sense, especially since the paw print didn't seem definitively tiger-ish to me. It was just closer to that than any of the other prints I'd seen on the website I'd checked.

I set the plaster cast of the print to one side, figuring I'd show it to Noah when he came over to check on Milo. Maybe he would know whether anyone in the area kept exotic cats as pets.

At the very least, he might be able to corroborate that the print really had come from a tiger, or from something else.

Thinking about Noah made me wonder if I dared ask him to stay for dinner again. It was early enough in the afternoon that I could throw a roast in the crockpot or something, even though I'd have to use a magical assist to get it defrosted in time, since the main component of that particular meal was still sitting in the freezer.

No, making that kind of offer would be horribly obvious. Ordering pizza the night before had been a spur-of-the-moment decision, whereas if I had a pot roast and veggies just waiting for his arrival, he'd know something was up. I had absolutely no idea where any of this was headed, but making it seem as though I'd expected him to stay for dinner again would send up a whole host of red flags.

I'd have to play it by ear and see what happened.

However, just because I'd crossed pot roast off the list didn't mean there weren't plenty of other things I could do in the kitchen to keep me busy.

By the time five-thirty rolled around, I had a whole new batch of insomnia tinctures and my surefire arthritis remedy bottled up and ready to go. Of course, I couldn't claim that any of my elixirs were solutions to medical problems, but it was easy enough to make the labels vague and always include a disclaimer about how they weren't intended as pharmaceuticals and to consult your doctor, blah, blah. I knew the stuff worked, and so did my customers, because they always came back for more, but I also knew I needed to make sure I covered my butt just in case.

Milo snored his way through all of this, and didn't wake up until the doorbell rang at a little past five-thirty. Sure enough, that was Noah on the doorstep, looking as casually gorgeous as ever, thick brown hair slightly mussed after a day of working with his animal patients. Today he wore a chambray shirt that echoed the color of his eyes, along with a somewhat rumpled pair of khakis.

"How's our patient doing?" he asked as I let him into the living room.

"Much better," I replied. "See for yourself."

Because of course Milo had gotten out of bed as soon as he heard the doorbell, and now his tail was wagging furiously after recognizing who the visitor was. Noah squatted down to pet him...and also to take a peek under his bandages.

"Looks like everything's healing great," he said. "How're you feeling, boy?"

In response, Milo gave a short, happy bark, tail still going like crazy.

"He slept most of the day," I said. "But his appetite was good, and he was fine with going out in the backyard, although he had to be careful walking down the steps."

"That all sounds really good." Noah got back up and then sent me a careful glance. "Everything quiet around here?"

"Very quiet," I responded. "But there's something I want you to take a look at." I went over to the coffee table and retrieved the plaster cast of the paw print I'd taken a few hours earlier. "I got this off a print I found in the backyard, and when I looked it up on a paw print identification site, it looked like it might have come from a tiger."

"'A tiger'?" Noah repeated, looking a little stunned.

"I think so." I handed him the little piece of plaster. "But I could be wrong. I'm no expert."

For a moment, he was quiet as he studied the rounded outlines of the paw print. Then he asked, "Can you show me the site where you looked it up?"

"Sure."

The laptop was still resting on the coffee table, so I sat on the couch and opened it up. The animal print identification site's tab was open on my browser, making it easy enough to click on the site and then swivel the screen toward Noah.

He came over and sat down next to me—not too close, but definitely close enough that I could smell the clean scent of soap on his hands and see the faint dusting of dark stubble on his cheeks. My heartbeat wanted to speed up, and I told it to take a rest. I couldn't deny the effect the man had on me, but the last thing I wanted was for him to notice that I saw him as just a little more than my friendly neighborhood vet.

After putting the plaster cast of the print down on the table in front of us, he said, "Do you mind?" and reached for the laptop.

"No, go ahead," I told him, and handed over the MacBook. It wasn't as if I had anything incriminating open on there, only my email and a site that stocked apothecary supplies, where I was planning to re-order some bottles and stoppers.

For a moment, he was silent as he scanned the contents of the screen, the diagrams that compared the paw prints of the various big cats to one another, aided by actual photos of those animal tracks in the wild. Then he shook his head and gave the laptop back to me.

"I'm not sure," he said at length. "The shape is a little off...the prints are rounded, but not rounded enough to be a tiger's. Even if they are from a tiger, who in the world would sic a wild cat like that on a domestic dog?"

About all I could do was give a helpless lift of my shoulders. "I have no idea," I replied. "I was hoping you might know if anyone around here had a pet tiger."

"No," he responded at once, which was about what I'd expected. "It's illegal to own wild or exotic animals in the state of Massachusetts. You can apply for a permit, but those permits aren't given out very often, and I know there isn't anyone in Salem who has any kind of wild animal, let alone a big cat."

Although none of this was a huge surprise, it only increased the mystery. Clearly, someone had released something in my yard for the sole purpose of attacking Milo. I would have wondered how they got onto the property at all, since I made sure to keep up my protection spells even when I wasn't worried about wild animals roaming the area.

But the fence on the east side of my property was supposed to be maintained by my neighbors, and they hadn't done a very good job of keeping it in good repair. I knew for a fact that there were several gaps where an animal could get through. It hadn't been a concern when I was letting Milo out in the yard, mostly because he wasn't your typical dog and I'd known he wouldn't try to wander.

And since the Davidsons were away at the moment, traveling Maryland in their RV so they could visit their kids and grandkids, I knew for a fact that it probably would have been pretty easy to back into their driveway and release an animal without anyone noticing. We were a fairly tight-knit community out here on Winter Island Drive, but most of my neighbors would have been at work while the dirty deed was going down.

I explained all this to Noah—omitting the part

about the protection spells on my property—and he gave a grim nod.

"Yes, that makes sense," he said, even as his gaze strayed toward Milo, who'd lain down on the rug nearby so he could listen to our conversation. "Or at least, the mechanics of how it happened make sense. What I don't understand is why anyone would make Milo the target of that kind of attack."

On the surface, maybe not. But someone had killed Darla Fitzgerald, and it didn't take too huge a leap of the imagination for me to think the murderer might have decided the dog was also a threat and needed to be eliminated. Milo was a familiar, after all, and therefore no ordinary house pet. He would have been privy to Darla's secrets— maybe not all of them, because of the way she seemed to have kept her familiar at arm's length, but still—and possibly one of those secrets had been enough to make someone commit murder.

"I have no idea," I lied, and Noah frowned.

"You should really call the police," he said next.

Contacting the authorities was just about the last thing I wanted to do. In the first place, I had a feeling they wouldn't even believe the attack was premeditated, despite the physical evidence that a wild animal of some kind really had been prowling around my backyard. Oh, they'd probably reach out to contact anyone in the state who had a permit for such a beast, but what good would that do? I had to believe anyone who would use an exotic pet to carry out such an attack wouldn't even have the animal registered.

Also, those of us in the witch world did whatever we could to avoid attracting any attention from the law enforcement community, because the last thing we wanted was anyone in a position of authority to start nosing around and maybe discover there was something odd about all those nice ladies in their black dresses. That was why witches tended to be law-abiding in the extreme, leading quiet lives that didn't invite any scrutiny.

"And what do you think the police would do to help?" I asked, and Noah looked a little uneasy.

"They could ask around, at least," he responded.

"I've lived in this town my entire life," I told him. "Maybe there's someone around who's keeping a tiger or whatever, but honestly, I think the most exotic animals inside Salem's town limits are Chuck Hansen's alpacas. I can't really see them going on a rampage and trying to take a chunk out of someone's cocker spaniel."

Despite the seriousness of the situation, Noah grinned at my remark, a smile that made me glad I was sitting down, since it made my knees feel all wobbly.

I really needed to get a grip.

"You're right about that," he said. "Although

his newest alpaca, Daisy, always tries to take a bite out of my shirt whenever I make a house call."

As far as I was concerned, Daisy could munch away all she liked. My thoughts went to very dangerous places when I tried to imagine Noah Jenkins shirtless.

"Anyway," I said, "It's been really quiet lately, so I'm starting to think this whole thing must have been some kind of a terrible accident. Maybe someone was traveling through town and their tiger or whatever it was got loose and went after Milo before they were able to capture it again."

A single raised eyebrow told me Noah didn't put much credence in that theory. Well, neither did I, since I was sure the whole thing had been deliberate. However, as much as I liked having him help with Milo and come by to make house calls to check on him, I knew there was no way in the world I could ever tell Noah the truth about what was going on.

Especially since I only had a few random facts to work with so far, nothing that told me exactly why Darla was dead, or why her familiar had been targeted in such a terrible way.

To my relief, though, Noah only said, "Well, I suppose that makes as much sense as anything else. All the same, I'm going to try asking some of my vet friends in Boston if they know of anyone who keeps wild cats as pets. That might help us figure out what really happened."

"Sure, that sounds like a good idea," I agreed, and Noah seemed ready to leave matters there. He got up from the couch, and I rose as well.

"Milo's doing great," he said. "I don't think I need to keep checking on him every day, but it's probably a good idea if you bring him into the clinic later this week just so I can make sure he's still on the road to recovery."

I nodded, doing my best to ignore the stab of disappointment that went through me at those words. Of course I couldn't expect Noah to keep dropping by the house...even though I really wished he would.

"That sounds fine," I replied, trying to sound cheery and not at all as though he'd just thrown a figurative bucket of cold water over me. "Maybe on Thursday afternoon?"

"Okay. I don't have any appointments after four, so any time after that."

Well, it was better than nothing. I'd already resolved to bring Milo to work with me once I thought he'd be all right leaving the house, and considering how quickly he seemed to be healing, it looked as though I'd be able to do that the very next day. And Thursday was the day after that, so it wasn't as if I'd have to be waiting weeks and weeks to see Noah.

Before I could respond, he spoke again, now sounding almost diffident. "But um...maybe you'd want to have dinner on Wednesday night? If you don't want to leave Milo alone, I understand."

About all I could do was stand there and blink.

Had Noah Jenkins just asked me out on a *date?*

Milo sat up and tilted his head, and his tail whisked across the polished oak floor. From what I could tell, he definitely wanted me to go out with his veterinarian.

Before Noah could interpret my stunned silence as a refusal, I said quickly, "Wednesday night would be great. I can get someone to come watch Milo, or maybe we could go someplace where we could eat outside and I could bring him along?"

For a moment, I thought I might have overstepped my bounds with that request, but then Noah smiled, saying, "That's a great idea. How about Mercy Tavern? I've heard it's good, but I've never been there."

Considering Mercy was one of my favorite places to eat, he couldn't have chosen a better venue for our first date. Also, the food was good but it wasn't fancy, which meant there wouldn't be the same pressure as there might if we went to some kind of fine dining establishment. And it had a great pet-friendly patio.

"Mercy Tavern would be great," I said.

"Then I'll pick you up tomorrow at seven." Noah bent and ruffled Milo's ears, adding, "And I'll see you, too, Milo."

That seemed to be that, although Noah also reminded me to call him if there was any change in his patient's condition. Then he was gone, promising again that he'd see me at seven the following night.

I shut the door, feeling just a bit too tingly all over.

Maybe I wasn't any closer to finding out who had killed Darla Fitzgerald and who'd coordinated that awful attack on Milo, but things were still definitely looking up.

Chapter 9

Thick as Thieves

MILO SEEMED HAPPY THAT I'D BE SPENDING more time with Noah, and also was just fine with coming to work with me the next day.

"I'll get to see lots of new people, right?" he asked, and I scratched him behind the ear.

"Lots and lots," I promised. "It should be fun."

Or at least, I hoped it would be. I'd already texted Sage to let her know I'd be bringing the dog with me to the shop, and she replied that she was looking forward to meeting him. So far, I hadn't told her anything about the tiger or whatever it was, and I wasn't sure whether I even would. She was a great assistant, but I didn't want to completely freak her out, especially when it seemed as though the wild animal responsible for the wounds on my newly adopted dog had long since left the area.

Tuesday night was quiet, with Milo snuggled next to me on the couch as I watched TV. He definitely appeared to be improving by leaps and bounds, but I didn't see the need to tire him out with too much activity, especially when he was going to be spending the whole next day at the store with me.

And after he'd curled up at the foot of the bed, nose on the afghan I always had spread there even though I definitely didn't have any need of it at this time of year, I went to the window to look outside. From my bedroom, I had a clear view of Juniper Cove, quiet and serene under a nearly full moon. If anything was moving out there, it had to be small, because the landscape seemed utterly still, with not even a breeze from the ocean to rustle the leaves on the trees.

Yes, that wild animal definitely wasn't coming back. Maybe the whole thing really had been a terrible accident.

Every instinct I possessed, though, told me the attack had been deliberate. That Milo had survived at all seemed like a complete miracle.

Or maybe not exactly a miracle. The protective enchantments I had placed on the house might not have been enough to prevent the assault, but they could have kicked in to make sure the dog didn't share his mistress's fate.

And we seemed to be safe now. There was

nothing on the property that meant us any harm, so I knew I should be able to sleep without fear. After all, it had been quiet here yesterday evening as well.

I went back to bed and climbed under the covers. Milo shifted slightly but didn't seem inclined to get down from the bed.

And that was fine. Even though I told myself I shouldn't be worried, I couldn't help thinking there was safety in numbers, so it was probably smarter for him to stay up here with me.

Tomorrow would be even better, because then we'd be at the store...and afterward, we'd have dinner with Noah on the patio at Mercy Tavern.

With those comforting thoughts to reassure me, I allowed myself to drift off to sleep.

"He's just gorgeous!" Sage exclaimed, bending down so she could pat Milo on the head. "But it's so awful that something attacked him."

"He's been a trooper through the whole thing," I said, smiling as I watched the dog cheerfully submit to my assistant's caresses. "The vet said he was okay to go out, which is why I thought I'd bring him along today."

Even though Sage didn't know anything about my secret attraction to Noah Jenkins—and although she probably thought he was way too old for her—her mouth twisted a bit in barely concealed amusement at my casual reference to "the vet." Salem wasn't so big that a veterinarian who looked like he modeled for *GQ* in his spare time could be easily overlooked.

However, she obviously decided it was better not to comment, because she said, "Yes, getting out and seeing people is probably a good thing for Milo. But if he gets too tired, it's fine if you have to take him home. I can cover for you if that happens."

"We'll see how it goes," I said lightly. I had every intention of spending the whole day here, but it was still nice to know Sage was willing to watch the store once again if I ended up having to take Milo back to the house because he'd over-exerted himself.

My assistant nodded, then headed into the storeroom to unpack the boxes of tinctures and elixirs I'd brought with me, the fruit of my forced stay at home the past couple of days. I'd asked her to do that so I could spend some time up front with Milo, who now seemed intent on wandering around the space and drinking in all the new sights and scents.

"This is a very interesting-smelling place," he announced when he came back to the front of the store, where I was just unlocking the door.

I didn't have to worry about anyone over-hearing us talking, because I was the only person in the world—now that Darla Fitzgerald was gone, anyway—who could understand what the dog was saying. To anyone else, it would merely sound as though he was whining a little, or possibly letting out a very small bark. And if a customer caught me talking to Milo, well, it wasn't as if I was the only person in the world who had in-depth conversations with her dog.

"There are lots of interesting things here, true," I said. Because it was such a nice day, sunny and bright, with only a few clouds lazily drifting in off the ocean, I decided to prop open the door with the little cast-iron hedgehog I used for that very purpose. "Just remember to pay attention to how our customers are acting. If they're friendly, that's great, but if it seems clear they don't like dogs or want to shop without anyone bothering them, then you need to keep your distance."

"I know that," Milo returned, sounding a little offended that I'd believe he wasn't capable of minding his manners while working with the public. "You know I won't get underfoot."

"Yes, I do," I said, and bent down so I could scratch him behind one of his soft, floppy ears. "You're very good about that. Let me show you where I put your food and water."

Tail wagging, he followed me to the little break

room in the back of the shop, really just an empty space containing a small table and two chairs shielded by a Japanese folding screen, along with a tiny apartment-sized microwave on top of an old rolling stand I'd repurposed here after I redid my kitchen. Next to the microwave stand was a spot for Milo's bowls, while I'd squeezed his bed into a corner.

"You can come back here and lie down any time you're feeling tired," I said, and the dog went over and sniffed at his bed, apparently satisfying himself that it was the same bed he'd been sleeping in for the past two days. Then he drank a little water, and gave a satisfied nod.

"It's nice spot," he said. "I know I can sleep back here."

I hadn't expected him to protest the setup, but it was still nice to know the makeshift arrangement met his approval. The two of us went past Sage, who was currently making space on the storeroom shelves for the new stock I'd brought, and then back out front.

It didn't look as though we'd had any customers yet, which wasn't too surprising. On quiet weekdays like this, things often didn't pick up until after lunch, when people wanted to get out and browse while they were digesting their midday meals. I took advantage of the current calm to get out a duster and clean off some of the bottles behind the counter, and to quickly take a look at the stock on display to make sure nothing had gotten put back out of place. Sage tried to stay on top of that sort of thing, but when she was forced to work solo the way she had the past couple of days, it was inevitable that a few things would escape her notice.

However, our stock was in better order than I'd feared, so it didn't take me very long to tidy up the few items that weren't where they were supposed to be. Off to one side, Milo watched me with some curiosity, telling me he'd probably never been in a shop quite like mine before. Darla might have been a witch, but since she'd also owned a PR firm and seemed like a very practical sort of person, I sort of doubted she'd ever set foot in a place like Full Moon Apothecary.

"What do all those things do?" he asked.

Since Sage was still in the stockroom, and it looked as though we might not get any customers before lunch, I didn't have a problem replying to the dog's question.

"All sorts of things," I said. "Some of these elixirs help people with their achy joints, and some help them sleep better. And several of them are just to make a person feel better overall, to boost their energy levels." I paused there and decided it was finally time to ask the question that had been plaguing me ever since I found a wounded Milo in my backyard. Before now, I hadn't wanted to bother him, knowing he needed to rest more than anything else, but today he seemed to be back to his usual self, despite the bandages on his throat and paws. "How in the world did you ever fight off that tiger?"

The dog sat back on his haunches and reached up to scratch at an ear. "It wasn't a tiger."

I blinked. "It wasn't?"

"No," Milo replied. "I don't know what it was. I'd never seen anything like it, even on TV. It was big and fast and had dark fur."

"A bear?" I asked next, knowing I sounded dubious. Those prints I'd found hadn't looked exactly like anything in particular, but they definitely hadn't been from a bear.

"Nope," the dog said. He didn't seem particularly troubled by the possibility that he'd been attacked by something he couldn't identify. "Like I said, I don't know what it was. It smelled weird, too."

"Weird how?" I asked, after glancing toward the shop's front window to make sure no customers were about to appear and interrupt our conversation.

"I don't know. Just weird. Not like an animal, but not like a person, either."

Well, this whole thing kept getting better and better. I supposed it was possible Milo had been so focused on fighting off his attacker that the impressions he'd gotten during the encounter were completely off-base, but an inner instinct told me that theory wasn't correct.

"But it's okay," Milo went on. "I fought it off. I really think what probably helped was the protection spell Darla cast on me."

I stared at him, pushing the identity of the strange attacker to the back of my mind so I could focus on the dog's words. "You never said anything about a protection spell to me."

"You didn't ask."

Well, that was true. And since dogs tended to be very "in the moment" kinds of creatures, it probably wouldn't have even occurred to him to mention the spell until it came up.

I had to wonder why Darla Fitzgerald would have found herself compelled to do such a thing, especially when it seemed as though she wasn't terribly thrilled about having a familiar in the first place. However, I didn't want to ask the question directly, mostly because it would have sounded rude.

Instead, I inquired, "When did she do that?"

"The day before she brought me to stay with you."

Interesting. Once again, I got the feeling that Darla had somehow been aware of her impending doom, and had decided she needed to add an extra layer of protection to her canine charge, especially since he was going to stay with a stranger.

There was no way to know for sure, of course. About all I could do was be very, very glad that the spell had held and Milo had escaped with his life, if not completely unscathed.

And while some might have wondered why Darla hadn't cast the same kind of spell to protect herself, I knew it wasn't quite that easy. It was much, much harder for witches to create enchantments that worked on themselves, which was partly why it was a lot easier for me to cast a "look someplace else" spell when I was up to something witchy that I didn't want seen by a mundie, rather than try to turn invisible. There were exceptions to every rule—my friend Stella was very good at making herself undetectable to the naked eye—but in general, a witch couldn't give herself the same protections Darla had provided for Milo.

That was why I cast all my protection spells on my house and on my yard. They were separate from me, but putting those extra layers of security in place accomplished nearly the same thing.

I didn't know why Darla hadn't done the same for her condo, something that would have repelled anyone seeking to come in and cause her any mischief. No witch was invincible, though, and I supposed it was possible she'd already stretched herself thin by casting first the silence spell on Milo and then the protection enchantment that followed.

"Well," I said lightly. "It's a very good thing she did that. And it looks as though you put up quite a fight."

"I did," the dog replied, sitting up a little straighter, chin lifted proudly. "Although I sort of got the feeling the creature wasn't very good at attacking people. As soon as I bit it on the arms, it ran away and jumped over the fence."

Also interesting. Was that Milo's protection spell at work, or had something else been going on?

Because I couldn't exactly sit down with the thing...whatever it was...and get its recounting of the events of that particular Monday afternoon, I had to take Milo's word for it.

"That's because you're a big tough guy," I said, and went over so I could ruffle his ears. His tail wagged happily, making it obvious to me that he hadn't suffered any lasting scars from the encounter, and in fact was proud of himself for sending his attacker running.

Or...had he? Was it the spell, or the possibility that the beast didn't have much stomach for a direction confrontation when it turned out its victim wasn't as defenseless as it had thought?

So many questions, so few answers. For now, though, I was just glad that the dog was on the mend, and I was back at work, surrounded by the comforting sights and smells of my store.

It also felt like a safe space.

As I'd thought, business picked up after lunch, and Sage and I were kept occupied by waiting on customers, explaining the contents of the various elixirs and tonics and what they could do for a person. Through all this, Milo behaved himself very well, and stayed on his bed in the back corner of the shop when it became apparent the small space couldn't accommodate that many patrons and a dog underfoot as well.

I'd taken him for a walk at lunch when I went out to grab sandwiches for Sage and me, so I knew he should be all right until I was able to take a break sometime in the middle of the afternoon. In fact, I'd told him as much and he seemed to accept the situation, although he didn't look too thrilled at the realization that he'd have stay out of the way for a few more hours.

His droopy expression made me feel a bit guilty, although I told myself the dog was much safer here with me, and that he would have been even more bored at the house. At least here he had people around and got to go on a walk, while if he'd stayed behind he would have had to hold it for much longer, since my home didn't have a doggie door.

"Do you have anything for insomnia?" a man asked, someone who'd just walked in.

"Sure," I said, assuming the usual cheery smile I wore when working with customers. "Do you have trouble falling asleep, or do you wake up in the middle of the night?"

"Falling asleep," the man said promptly.

He looked as though he was probably about ten years or so older than I, with medium brown hair and hazel eyes. Something about him seemed vaguely familiar, although I was pretty sure I'd never seen him before. But then, I occasionally had that feeling of *déjà vu* when customers came in, just because people weren't as unique as they liked to think they were, and it wasn't that uncommon to run across a person who reminded me of someone else.

And since this man seemed fairly average— middle height and build, attractive in an unassuming sort of way—I could see why I might think I'd seen him somewhere before.

"I have just the thing for you," I said, and turned so I could pull a bottle down from the shelf behind me. "All you have to do is put four or five drops in a glass of water and drink it right before you go to sleep. Works like a charm."

Which was only the truth. Like many of my

elixirs, the "Fast Sleep" potion had a small enchant-ment placed on it, this one to ensure quick, restful sleep, so even the worst case of insomnia was no match for it.

"I'll take one," the man said, and then glanced behind him at the racks of dried herbal mixtures and the small display of scented candles. "Mind if I browse a bit?"

"Take all the time you need," I told him as I set his sleep potion off to one side. "Just come back when you're ready to check out."

He nodded and moved off toward the back of the store. I lost sight of him after that, because a bus had just disgorged a group of tourists, mostly women, who swarmed into the shop and started asking questions about all the various bottles on the shelves behind me. In fact, both Sage and I were kept busy for at least the next fifteen minutes or so, and rang up hundreds of dollars in purchases.

It was only after the group moved on to the next shop—Witch City Wicks, a candle store—that I was able to take a breath. My gaze fell on the sleep elixir I'd set to one side, and I frowned.

"That man never came back for his bottle of Fast Sleep," I said, and Sage just grinned at me.

"He probably gave up after the horde descend-ed," she remarked, still smiling. "I think I would have bolted, too, if I'd had the chance."

While her explanation seemed logical enough,

it wasn't quite enough to dispel the niggling worry at the back of my mind. "I didn't see him leave," I pointed out, and Sage shrugged.

"Would you have even noticed with all those people crowding around?"

Maybe not. Since the two of us had been left alone—for the moment, at least—I stepped out from behind the counter and headed toward the back of the store. It wouldn't have been the first time someone helped themselves to an elixir here and a bag of herbs there while Sage and I were otherwise occupied, but as far as I could tell, nothing appeared to be missing.

Since it looked as though we were going to have a small break for the next few minutes, I decided to put the mystery of the missing customer at the back of my mind and instead take Milo for a walk. Like Sage had said, the shop had been extremely crowded, and I probably just hadn't noticed the man walking out.

Except when I went to the back corner behind the screen where I'd set up Milo's food and bowls and bed, the dog was nowhere to be seen.

"Milo?" I said, even as I realized it was ridiculous to call for him, since there was absolutely nowhere he could hide back here.

A cold trickle of worry shivered its way down my spine, even as I told myself not to get worked up about nothing. Just because I hadn't seen the dog as I was inspecting the racks didn't mean anything. We could have passed each other, after all.

There weren't that many aisles in the store, though, and the floors were wood. I should have at least heard his toenails clicking on the old oak, even if I hadn't spotted him.

"Is Milo up here?" I asked as I returned to the counter.

Sage shook her head. "No, I thought he was sleeping in the back."

"He was," I said. "But he's not there now."

Although she normally wore a cheerful expression only enhanced by her heart-shaped face and flash of a dimple, now my assistant looked just as worried as I felt.

"Well, he's got to be around here somewhere," she replied, then came out from behind the counter. "Milo!"

I really, really hoped I'd been fretting over nothing, and that the dog would appear, tail wagging and expression quizzical, as if he couldn't figure out why we were making such a fuss.

But no one came to answer Sage's call, and my heart sank even further. Where could he be?

"Maybe he got out," she suggested. "I mean, we had a lot of people leaving the shop at the same time. He could have slipped away in a big group or something."

If we were talking about a regular cocker spaniel, I might have believed that, since they were an energetic breed that loved to be out and about. But a familiar was an entirely different case, and now that it seemed as though Milo had bonded to me at least a little bit, I knew there was no way he'd voluntarily leave my side.

Then I remembered the man who'd asked for the sleep potion, and who'd claimed he wanted to wander around the shop and look some more. He'd disappeared toward the back of the space just as we were mobbed by that tour group, and I hadn't been able to see where he'd gone.

What if he'd slipped into the back where Milo was sleeping and grabbed him? He wouldn't have had to go out through the front, since there was a rear exit from the storeroom that opened onto a small parking area out back. If he'd left his car there, the man could have bundled the dog into his vehicle and been gone before Sage and I had any idea what was happening.

And then the answer snapped into place with shocking clarity.

The stranger who'd come into the shop was the man I'd seen in all those photos on Darla's hidden Facebook timeline. He'd looked different because his hair in person was darker, and he'd worn it differently, cut shorter, more severe.

A deliberate attempt to conceal his identity?

Lacking any other information, I had to believe that must be the case.

"I think the man who pretended to want a sleeping potion stole him," I said, and Sage looked at me as though I'd lost my mind.

"Why in the world would he take Milo?"

"Well, he's a valuable dog," I replied. "But I don't think that's it. I think that man had a connection to Darla Fitzgerald, although I'm not sure what it could be."

"Her boyfriend?" my assistant asked dubiously. Even though she hadn't met Darla, she clearly knew enough about the woman to believe Milo's former mistress didn't seem like the sort of person to be in a romantic relationship.

"I'm not sure," I said, doing my best to recall the contents of the photos I'd seen on Darla's Facebook account. She and the mystery man seemed to be having a good time together, but none of their poses had looked at all romantic.

No, there was something else going on here, even if I couldn't begin to guess what it might be.

"You should call the police," Sage said next, echoing Noah's words of the day before.

"We can't talk to the police," I replied, reflecting that my assistant had a lot to learn about how the witch world worked. Or maybe she'd decided the situation was dire enough that we needed to ignore the usual precautions.

Sage's shoulders slumped, and she gave a reluctant nod. "Maybe not. Then what are you going to do?"

"I'm not sure," I said. "But I'm getting that dog back, one way or another."

Chapter 10

A Flying Chance

I HATED TO MAKE THE PHONE CALL— canceling my first date with Noah Jenkins definitely wasn't on my list of fun things to do with my time—but it had to be done.

"Charity," he said, sounding surprised.

Of course he was surprised. He didn't have any reason to think he'd be doing anything other than picking me up at seven, as we'd planned.

"I can't make it tonight," I said. "Something's come up."

"Is everything okay?"

The obvious concern in his voice only made things worse. Around Sage, who was eight years younger than I and a lot less experienced about the world, I could be tough and brave and vow that I'd come up with a plan to locate Milo.

A sympathetic Noah Jenkins, on the other

hand, only made me want to break down in a blub-
bery mass of tears.

"Um, not really," I replied. "Milo is missing."

"'Missing'?" Noah repeated, his tone sharpen-
ing. "What happened?"

"I'm not sure," I said, then hesitated. Should I
tell him about my suspicions, or just try to make
this seem as if we were only dealing with a dog
who'd gone missing in an unfamiliar place?
Although I hated lying, I also knew I didn't want
to put Noah in any danger. "He's just gone."

"Okay," he said. His tone had shifted, and now
he sounded brisk and businesslike. "What do you
need me to do?"

I blinked. Although I'd assumed he'd probably
be sympathetic, I honestly hadn't thought he'd
offer to help. "Um...what can you do?"

"Well, if you can get me some photos of Milo, I
can put them up here in the clinic in case anyone
has seen him."

That would have been a great idea...except I
didn't have any pictures of the dog. I wasn't the
sort of person who always had her phone handy
and was taking pictures of anything and everything, right down to my morning cup of tea and
slice of toast. Also, I hadn't seen a single shot of
him on Darla's Facebook wall, or I could have gone
there and snagged at least one picture.

And she must have had a phone, but I had to

believe it was currently sealed up in an evidence locker, unless the police had decided to release her effects to her family. I knew absolutely nothing about them except they also lived in Chicago, and yet I had to believe that, even if I was able to dig up their phone number somewhere, they'd think I was crazy if I tried to ask them whether they had any photos of Milo.

Or maybe not. Just because she hadn't been particularly close to the dog didn't mean Darla's mother might not have wanted some photos of her daughter's familiar.

No matter their feelings on the subject, it would take me a whole lot of time to try tracking them down, and in the meantime, Milo was in the clutches of a man who clearly wanted him for some nefarious purpose.

"I don't have any," I said miserably.

"That's all right," Noah responded at once. "I can look up pictures online of English cocker spaniels and see if I can find one that's close. We'd have to add some information about how he has a bandage on his throat anyway, so I think that should still work." A pause, and he added, "If you want, I can come over after my last appointment and drive around town with you. Maybe he just got out and wasn't sure how to get home, since he's in a new place."

"I tried that," I said. Or at least, after Sage had

told me she'd watch the shop for the rest of the afternoon, I'd zigged and zagged on my way home, hoping against hope that maybe I'd spot Milo's golden-furred form roaming down one of those streets, but I hadn't seen a single sign of him.

"The whole town?" Noah persisted, obviously undeterred. "We can go look for him, and grab some takeout and bring it back to the house so we'll have some fortification while we're putting together lost-dog flyers."

Despite how terrible the situation was, I couldn't help cheering up slightly at his offer. It seemed as though he was determined for us to have an evening together, even if it might not have been the dinner out we'd had planned.

"Okay," I said. "That could work. And I'll put out the word among all my friends to keep an eye out for him."

"Then I'll be over a little after five. Just hang in there."

"I will," I promised. "And—thank you, Noah."

"It's the least I can do."

We ended the call there, but I didn't put down my phone. Normally, I would have called my mother first, figuring she could pass along the necessary information through our local witch network, but I knew she'd gone down to Boston for the day with Valerie Monroe, Stella's grandmother.

I wasn't without resources, though. Instead, I called Grace Bowersby, gave her the scoop, and did my best to provide a description of the man who'd taken Milo.

"Unfortunately, he's not very remarkable," I said. "But when I saw him, he was wearing a black polo shirt and jeans. Hopefully, that will help."

"We're on it," Grace replied. "Don't you worry —we'll find him."

I thanked her, and we ended the call after that. Under most circumstances, I would have bet good money there was no way the man would be able to evade a bunch of witches trying to track him down, but he was obviously slippery. Since every instinct I possessed told me that "Dave Michaels" wasn't the man's real name, and I'd already discovered he was very good at hiding his identity from Google and everyone else, I didn't know how much luck Salem's witches were going to have.

Waiting for Noah to get off work was excruciating, although I tried to keep my spirits up by reassuring myself that Darla's protection spell would keep Milo from any physical harm.

Except...what if it didn't? What if it had begun to wear off, just as the spell she'd cast to prevent him from speaking had also eventually faded away?

As much as I wanted to dismiss that horrible idea, I couldn't quite ignore it. Some minor spells could go on and on without needing much refreshing, like the magical screen on my back door, while others needed to get a boost from time to time in order to ensure they would continue as originally cast.

Protection spells weren't minor.

To keep myself from completely climbing the walls, I went outside to the garden and gathered some herbs. The sunlight on my hair and the warm smells from the various blooming plants made me feel a little better, but not much.

Why would that man have kidnapped Milo? Even though he was no ordinary dog, it wasn't as though he'd be of any use to a regular human— beyond his intrinsic value as a purebred, desirable animal.

And yet, since the stranger clearly had a connection to Darla, I had to believe this had nothing to do with an English cocker spaniel's value on the black market.

No, Milo had been taken for a specific reason.

After I finished bundling the herbs and hanging them on the rack that dominated one wall of the kitchen, I went back outside and wandered through the garden, trying to see if there was a piece of evidence I'd overlooked, something left behind from the animal attack that might provide an additional clue. Unfortunately, I didn't find a damn thing. Even the paw prints were gone, blurred by what looked to have been the passage of a group of rabbits overnight.

But I'd killed enough time that Noah should be over in just a few more minutes. I hurried upstairs and combed my hair, then applied some lip gloss. Putting on anything other than the black top and jeans I'd worn to work would have looked way too obvious, especially considering we were about to go out and start searching for a lost dog, so I settled for smoothing the hem of the blouse and hoping I looked socially acceptable enough for something that wasn't quite a first date.

Yes, it was probably silly to be worried about that kind of thing when Milo could be in mortal danger, but if nothing else, fretting about something so minor helped to distract me during those last few moments.

Noah was right on time, ringing the doorbell just a few minutes after four-thirty. He didn't bother with any pleasantries, but only said, "I got over here as fast as I could. Have you heard anything?"

"No," I replied. "I put out the word on the local w—" I stopped myself there, realizing I was so harried I'd almost slipped and said "local witch network," and course-corrected with, "—women's group my mom is active with. Everyone's going to be watching for him."

"Well, that's good news. Are you ready to go?"

I nodded, and slipped my purse over my shoulder. A pause as I locked the door behind me—it wasn't really necessary, considering all the protection spells I had laid on the house, but I knew Noah would expect it—and then we hurried down the front path to the spot where his white pickup truck was waiting at the curb.

He opened the door for me and I got in, then waited while he went around the truck to the driver's side and climbed into his seat. "I thought we'd head toward the North River and look around there first. It's not too far from your shop, and cockers like water. Lots of interesting smells over there."

Under normal circumstances, I would have thought this was a good idea. However, Milo wasn't simply a dog who'd gotten bored and decided to go exploring, but instead had been forcibly taken from my store.

Problem was, I couldn't tell Noah any of that. It wasn't that I didn't trust him, but only that the motivations for the dognapping must have had something to do with the witchy world, and I absolutely had to keep our world secret from outsiders...even an outsider like Noah Jenkins.

I allowed myself a nod. "Sure, let's start there."

Just the briefest sideways glance, as though Noah had picked up on the skeptical tone in my voice but wasn't sure what to do about it. To my relief, though, he didn't say anything, only started the engine and pulled away from the curb.

Once we were driving down Fort Avenue, headed toward town, he spoke. "There's some flyers we put together in that folder there."

He inclined his head toward a manila folder sitting on the front seat, something I hadn't noticed at first because a square Kleenex box had been placed directly on top of it. I moved the tissues out of the way and picked up the folder, then looked inside. There was a stack of paper with color laser-printed images of a golden-hued English cocker spaniel and the words "LOST DOG" written in hundred-point type at the top of each page. Beneath the dog's picture was a brief blurb about Milo, including the information that he had bandages on his throat.

"I put your phone number on there," Noah went on, now sounding almost apologetic. "I hope that's okay."

"Yes, it's fine," I said at once. "And the flyers look great. Thanks so much for doing that."

And I meant it. His original plan had made it sound as if he thought the two of us would create the flyers, but these looked a lot more professional than anything I could have done. Sage was usually the one who created ads for the store and any kind of flyers, since her graphic design skills were definitely more advanced than mine.

Noah sent me a sheepish glance before returning his attention to the road. "Well, actually, one of my lab techs did those for me. She's a lot better at that kind of thing than I am. We put one up on the bulletin board in my office, and I figured we could post the rest of them while we were out driving around."

"That's a great idea," I told him. And it was. I didn't think driving all over Salem and looking for Milo was probably going to help much—I had a feeling he and his dognapper were long gone—but if anyone had spotted the stranger with my dog and then saw one of the flyers, they'd realize the man had no right to be with the animal and would call me to let me know where they'd seen him.

At least, that was the hopeful scenario I allowed to play out in my head. Whether it would work that way in real life was a different question altogether.

We headed to Furlong Park, since it had decent parking that would allow us to leave Noah's truck behind while we went and roamed. Also, the ball field and the playground there were popular destinations, and a good place to post a flyer or two. After we'd hung those—he'd thoughtfully brought along a roll of masking tape for that part of the job —we walked toward the water's edge, calling Milo's name, keeping a sharp lookout for the dog.

Naturally, we didn't see him. We did bump

into a guy who was out walking a pair of beagles—who both wanted to jump up on our legs and be our new best friends—and we handed over a flyer, explaining we were out looking for a lost dog. The man scanned the flyer and told us he'd let us know if he saw Milo, and that made me feel a bit better. Not because I thought he'd actually spot my lost familiar, but because now I felt as though I had someone else in Salem besides the witch community keeping watch for the stolen animal.

After we roamed about a half mile or so along the river, we headed back to Noah's truck and drove around to more likely places, including another park and even the cemetery, the rationale being that the dog probably would have been attracted to open, green spaces. But we didn't see hide nor hair of him, so, since we'd either posted or given out all the flyers and it was beginning to get dark, we headed back to my house. On the way, we made a brief detour to grab some takeout from Spitfire tacos, but still, we were back and sitting at my dining table at a little before eight.

"I'm sorry we couldn't find him," Noah said, and he looked about as worried as a man could who'd just taken a bite of the restaurant's famous "vampiro" tacos, which were loaded with shaved steak, cheddar jack cheese, guacamole, and hot sauce. "But we'll keep looking."

It was on my lips to tell him it was okay, but of

course it wasn't. However, none of this was his fault, and he'd helped me as much as he could. And maybe...just maybe...we'd get really lucky, and someone actually might have spotted Milo and his kidnapper, and at least we'd have a vehicle description to go on.

Noah and I ate in silence for a few moments. I'd offered him beer or wine, but he'd declined, saying it had been kind of a long day and he'd rather just have water. While I thought I would have liked a glass of wine, I still understood. This day definitely felt as though it had been about a million years long.

The one highlight was being able to spend time with Noah. He'd gamely driven from place to place, handed out flyers, described Milo's bandages. Everyone we'd talked to had been sympathetic and promised to keep an eye out for the missing dog, which was all I could have asked for. Not once had he seemed annoyed with the process or upset that our first date was very different from what we'd planned, and I realized that not only was he very easy on the eyes, but was also a genuinely nice guy.

He paused now, though, and set his mostly eaten taco down on his plate. Fixing me with those brilliant blue eyes, he said, "Is there something you're not telling me, Charity?"

Oh, boy. Of course there was—about a hundred different "somethings," all of which I didn't dare divulge. I managed to swallow the bite of chicken taco I'd just taken, then responded, "What makes you say that?"

He didn't blink. "I don't know. Just a feeling. If it's something that'll help us find Milo, then I don't know why you'd keep it from me."

I wiped my fingers on the paper napkin in my lap, even as my mind raced. There had to be a way to tell him about Milo's kidnapper without mentioning that I was a witch...or that all the other pretend "witches" in Salem were just like me, and very, very real.

Yes, I could leave those parts out, and just say I thought something had been going on between Milo's former owner and the man I believed had taken him, even if I hadn't been able to puzzle out exactly what yet.

Noah continued to watch me, expression neutral. Would he be angry once he discovered I'd been keeping something from him, or would he understand why I'd felt the need to hold back a few pertinent facts?

Now I really wished I had a glass of wine in front of me. Since there was only water, though, I went ahead and had a sip to steady myself, then said, "I don't know for sure, because neither Sage nor I saw what really happened. But I'm really worried someone took Milo."

That revelation made Noah's eyes widen

slightly, but otherwise I didn't see much of a reaction. "What makes you say that?" he asked, tone remarkably calm, considering the circumstances.

Then again, he'd been trained to administer vaccines to hyperactive Jack Russell terriers and most likely had to force pills down squirming cats' throats on a daily basis, so he probably had plenty of experience keeping his cool, no matter what the circumstances.

So I described how the man had come into the shop and disappeared when Milo did, and how I didn't recognize him at first but then realized he had some kind of connection to Darla Fitzgerald.

"I didn't say anything before because I know how crazy this all sounds," I concluded. "But no one around here has seen Milo, and he's just not the kind of dog to take off like this."

Noah ran a hand over the stubble on his chin, and it looked as though he, too, was regretting the beer or glass of wine he'd refused half an hour earlier. "And yet you don't want to go to the police."

"What could they do?" I asked, hoping I didn't sound as desperate as I currently felt. The mere thought of Milo in that man's hands was enough to make my blood run cold, even as I tried to keep reassuring myself that Darla's protection spell was still in place and that we'd be able to rescue the dog before anything terrible happened. "I don't have any proof. I don't even think the guy's name is real. You really think the Salem police department is up to handling something like this?"

A long pause, and then Noah shook his head. "Probably not. They're fine as long as they're just dealing with a break-in or something, but in this case, I doubt they'd be able to do very much."

"Which puts us back to square one," I said glumly.

To my surprise, Noah didn't look quite as dejected as I was feeling right then. "Maybe not," he replied. "There's a guy I went to vet school with whose wife is a private detective. I can reach out to him and see if Ashley would be willing to do a little investigating for us."

Those words made me perk up immediately. True, private eyes weren't exactly infallible, but they had access to resources I certainly didn't. As I'd learned way too often in my life, witchy powers could only get you so far. Sometimes you really needed someone who knew which databases to hack.

"That would be amazing," I said. "Do you really think she'd help us out?"

"All I can do is ask," Noah said, but since he also looked a lot more cheerful than he had a few minutes earlier, I had to believe he thought his detective friend would decide to step in and offer some much-needed assistance. "But I know Ashley and Troy are serious dog people, so I have a feeling she'll want to take the case. I'll need screenshots, names, whatever you can give me, though."

"I can do that," I responded at once. "Do you mind hanging here while I get some stuff off my laptop?"

"No problem," Noah said as he reached for the remnants of his vampiro taco. "I think I can amuse myself."

Despite everything, I couldn't help grinning at his comment. Those Spitfire tacos were awfully good.

But the thought of my own taco waiting for me wasn't enough to keep me from hurrying out of the dining room and down the hall to my office. A couple of minutes to locate the cords I needed to attach my laptop to the color laser printer that sat on a nearby table, and then I took screencaps of every piece of Darla's Facebook timeline that featured a picture of David Michaels, as well as shots of her PR firm's website. Those were probably redundant, since Noah's private detective friend would be able to access it just fine with only the URL.

Still, I'd never worked with a private eye before, so I didn't know for sure what she might or might not need. Better to give her too much than not enough.

I returned to the dining room, sheaf of papers

in hand. The rest of Noah's taco was definitely gone, although I noticed he hadn't helped himself to another, even though three or four of them still waited in the bag of takeout we'd bought.

Cute and polite *and* thoughtful? It had been a long time since I'd been with anyone like him.

Actually, scratch that. I didn't think I'd ever met anyone like Noah Jenkins before, although I had to remind myself that I still didn't know very much about him. There was still plenty of time for all his bumps and awkward angles to reveal themselves.

I handed him the papers as I sat down again. "I hope this will help. But if it turns out there's anything else your friend's wife needs, just let me know."

He gave the papers a quick scan, then nodded. "This looks pretty substantial, but obviously, I'll let you know."

With that handled, he shifted the conversation to the tacos and other local restaurants, obviously doing his best to take my mind off the missing dog. I didn't know how successful he was, but I had to admit it was nice to hear him casually mention that we should still try to get to Mercy Tavern once the mess with Milo was handled, or maybe go to one of the town's numerous seafood restaurants.

If nothing else, it didn't look as though the

dognapping and its ensuing drama had been enough to scare Noah off.

After we were done, he helped me take the plates into the kitchen and drop the trash in the chrome garbage can I kept tucked away as discreetly as possible—because of the plumbing, there wasn't enough room to put one under the sink—and then he said, "Are you going to be okay?"

"I'm fine," I said stoutly, even though those words were mostly a lie. All through dinner, I'd kept wondering and worrying what was going on with Milo, whether his captor was treating him all right or whether he'd been shoved in a dark closet somewhere...or worse.

A corner of Noah's mouth twitched. "Okay, I'll let that go for now. But I just wanted to let you know that I did have a nice time, despite everything."

"Me too," I replied, and that was definitely the truth. If I hadn't had Noah's steady presence nearby to get me through the past couple of hours, I honestly didn't know what I would have done.

He reached out and took both my hands in his. His fingers felt a little rough—probably because of all the hand washing he had to do while on the job —but they were still strong and reassuring, utterly real. "It's going to be okay," he told me.

And then he bent down just a little and paused, as if asking permission.

At once, I lifted my face toward his, and in the next moment, our lips brushed against each other. He tasted a bit like hot sauce, and I thought it was probably the most delicious kiss I'd ever shared, one that made fun little thrills run up and down my spine.

For all my physical reaction, though, it was a chaste enough kiss, one that was barely open-mouthed, probably just about right for a first date that wasn't exactly a date.

Then he stepped away, expression on the borders of sheepish. "Maybe I shouldn't have done that, considering everything you've gone through today."

"No, it was exactly right," I replied, knowing I needed to disabuse him of the notion that our kiss had been a mistake. "I needed something to distract me."

Again, there was that utterly adorable quirk at the corner of his mouth. "Are you saying I'm distracting?"

"Very," I told him.

He leaned in for another kiss, a little deeper than the first one, but then he straightened and glanced at the sheaf of papers he held. "Well, I should probably get going. It's early enough that I think I can reach out to my friend Troy and explain the situation to him."

Even though part of me wanted Noah to stay in the kitchen and kiss me some more, a quick glance toward the clock on the stove told me it was only a little after eight, definitely not late enough that a text or a call would be too intrusive.

"That sounds like a good idea," I said.

After that exchange, there wasn't much left to do except walk him to the door, then stand there and watch as he made his way down the front path and got into his truck. He pulled away from the curb, but I didn't move until his taillights had disappeared around a curve in Winter Island Drive.

At last I put my fingertips to my mouth, head spinning slightly.

Noah Jenkins had kissed me, and was going to help me find Milo.

This was all going to work out just fine.

Chapter 11

Circle of Protection

I'D ONLY BEEN BACK INSIDE THE HOUSE FOR a couple of minutes when my cell phone rang. At once, I grabbed it and looked down at the screen, even though logic told me it was way too soon for Noah to have gotten home and contacted his veterinarian friend Troy and Troy's private detective wife, Ashley.

Sure enough, that wasn't Noah.

No, it was my mother.

"Hi, Mom," I said, marveling a little at how casual I sounded. Thank God, because I really didn't want to discuss Noah Jenkins when things between us were so fresh and new. It was bad enough that my mother had been needling me about settling down or maybe just going the donor route ever since I turned twenty-nine the previous

September. Maybe my biological clock was starting to tick now, but I still had plenty of time.

Or at least, I would if I had any intention of having a family. That was a discussion I'd purposely been avoiding, because I knew my mother would go right through the roof if she learned that our witchy line was going to stop with me. You'd think she would have figured it out by the way I always danced around the subject when she brought up settling down and having a baby, but maybe she simply wasn't ready to face the truth.

Then again, maybe she really did know deep down, but was also avoiding that particular confrontation for her own reasons.

"I just heard about Milo!" she exclaimed. "Why didn't you call me?"

"I didn't want to interrupt your time in Boston," I said. "Anyway, I don't think there's very much you could have done to help."

"There are lots of things," she declared. "At the very least, you could have asked me to cast a protection spell on you and the dog."

"He had one," I replied calmly. "Darla cast it on him before she died."

A brief silence followed that statement. But since it was my mother I was dealing with here, she wouldn't allow herself to remain deterred for very long. "How do you know the spell was even still in effect?"

"Because otherwise he would never have survived being attacked by a wild animal," I told her. "And that's why I have to think that spell is still protecting him now."

"Well, you don't know how long it's going to last," my mother said darkly. "Spells can continue after death, of course, but there's no way of knowing when this one is going to eventually run out."

Since I'd been worrying about exactly the same thing, it wasn't as though I could protest. Instead, I responded, "And that's why I'm doing everything I can to find him."

"Yes, I heard about the flyers...and how you were going all around town with Noah Jenkins." A pause, and her tone shifted subtly as she said, "How did you get *him* involved in all this?"

"Because he's the one who patched Milo up," I said. "He's worried about the dog, too."

"So worried that he went with you to Spitfire to get takeout and go back to your house?"

Not for the first time, I reflected that the CIA and the NSA had nothing on the witch network in my hometown. "We were hungry and tired after searching for Milo," I replied, knowing that response was just a teeny bit disingenuous. True, we'd needed some fortification after spending a couple of hours looking for the dog, but the date had been planned way before Milo was kidnapped.

But my mother didn't need to know that.

"I suppose so," she said, now sounding disappointed. But then her tone grew brisk as she went on, "Still, I think there's more we can do to help Milo. We should gather the coven and cast a new protection spell on him."

"We can do that without having him here with us?" I asked dubiously. I'd never heard of such a thing. Then again, just because I'd never heard of such a practice didn't mean it didn't exist. The world of magic and witchcraft was so deep and varied that no single witch could ever learn all of it in her lifetime.

"Working together, we can," my mother replied. "I'll call Valerie and Grace and a few of the others, and we can all meet at my house. Be here at nine o'clock."

Those words were issued as a command, not a suggestion, so I didn't bother to protest that I was tired and just wanted to sit down and put my feet up, and bask in the afterglow of Noah's kisses.

All right, I would have left that last part out, even if I'd had the guts to tell my mother I was exhausted and didn't want to go anywhere. After all, this was about Milo, not about me.

I guessed my mother wanted us to gather at her house because it was more centrally located than mine, and also because she had a dedicated space for spell circles and other kinds of magical workings in her basement. While my house had its own basement, I hadn't yet gotten around to fixing it up. Mostly, I used it to store holiday decorations and whatever other odds and ends wouldn't fit in my home's cupboards.

So I set down the phone and wearily climbed upstairs to brush my teeth and hair, and then refresh my lip gloss. Because it was my mother and she took these sorts of things seriously, I also changed out of my jeans and sleeveless top and into the black dress I usually wore for any summertime rituals, since it had short sleeves and therefore was better suited to warm weather.

And the hat, of course. Couldn't participate in a ritual with the coven without a tall, pointy hat. Unlike a lot of the other witches in town, I didn't wear it out and about much, and definitely not at work, because it just got in the way. For formal occasions, though, it was a requirement.

The hat rode on the front seat on the way over to my mother's house, though, because if I'd put it on my head, it would have scraped the roof of my Land Rover and been a general nuisance. Actually, I didn't put it on until I was safely inside, even though her neighbors on either side and across the street were also witches, and I wouldn't have attracted much notice.

After all these years, though, wearing the thing

still made me feel as if I should be out trick-or-treating or something.

Since I had the longest way to drive, I wasn't surprised that I was the last person to arrive at the house. Already waiting in my mother's living room were Valerie Monroe and Grace Bowersby, along with Elise Figg and Tonya Willis, my mom's neighbors.

That made six of us, more than enough to have some serious combined energy. The minimum for coven spell-casting was three, but it was definitely easier to scrape up a bunch of witches in Salem than it was in other parts of the world.

My mother came over and gave me a hug. Like me, she was a little more than average height, with bright red hair and clear gray eyes. Maybe that hair got a little help from Clairol these days, but because she'd always taken care to stay out of the sun, she looked a lot younger than sixty-two, more like someone in their early fifties, if even that much.

"I know you must be worried about Milo," she said. "But we'll soon put everything to rights." A glance past me as she added, "Are we all ready?"

The other women standing in the living room nodded. "We're ready," Grace said.

"Good."

No need to give them instructions as to what to

do next; we'd all done this plenty of times. Maybe not casting spells of protection, but we still gathered at the quarters of the year for our various rituals, and also to step in whenever someone in the community needed help, whether that was to ensure a bank loan came through or to give extra support to a witch suffering through a difficult pregnancy.

Our group of six headed down the stairs into the basement. Once upon a time, it had been a dull, dingy place, the walls unfinished and floor bare concrete, but my mother had expended a lot of effort to turn it into a welcoming space. Now the walls were covered in sheetrock and shaded a deep purple, and she'd painted constellations overhead on the black ceiling. The floor was warm maple, and sconces with faux candles flickered from every corner.

We formed a circle and joined hands. I had my mother on one side and Grace on the other, and I had to admit that feeling their fingers twined with mine made me a bit more hopeful about the situation, since I could sense the energy zinging through us, ready to be put to good use.

Since she'd called the coven together—and since she was the strongest witch of all of us—my mother took the lead. "We ask for your grace," she said, and the rest of us murmured her words.

"We ask for your grace."

"Give us the strength to send our power to Milo, an innocent."

Again, we echoed her words. This wasn't the spell itself, of course, but only those in our group calling upon the powers of the universe to give our magic the boost we needed to ensure the enchantment worked the way it was supposed to.

Then it was time to get down to business.

From the four quarters of the earth
From the four quarters of the year
From the sky above and the earth below
We draw your strength
We draw your comfort
We draw your power
Wrap it around Milo
Protect him from harm
Protect him from evil
Shield him and keep him safe
This we ask
This we command
So shall it be
So shall it be

This time, the magic swirling through the women in our circle was so strong that I could practically see it as a live thing, a creature of glitter and fire, ready to do our bidding to make sure Milo would come to no harm. It passed through all of us before moving upward and disappearing through the ceiling, presumably on its way to sheath itself around the dog in the magical equivalent of bubble wrap. No matter what David Michaels—or whatever his name was—tried to do to Darla Fitzgerald's former familiar, it wouldn't work.

Or at least, that was the theory. Since I didn't know where Milo was or what might be happening to him at the moment, I had to take all this on faith.

My mother, on the other hand, looked happy with the results of the spell, and sent a satisfied glance around the circle. "Well done," she said. "Now it's time to do the same thing for Charity."

Startled, I stared at her. "I thought this was about Milo."

"It was," she replied, unperturbed. "We've taken care of him, and we need to take care of you, too. I can't forget that that awful man went right into your shop to steal the dog. What if he decides to come back and get you, too?"

I opened my mouth to say that troubling scenario didn't seem very likely, but then shut it again just as quickly. After all, if Dave Michaels really had killed Darla, then there didn't seem to be too much he wasn't capable of. Having a little extra protection was probably a good thing.

So I gave a resigned nod and then released my mother's and Grace's hands, and let them re-form the circle. It might not be quite as powerful with five witches as it had been with six, but it should still be enough to give me some much-needed extra help.

And right then, I had a feeling I needed all the help I could get.

The spell was nearly the same as the one they'd cast for Milo, with a few subtle differences, since they were dealing with a human and not a dog. When it was done, I didn't feel much different. However, I'd seen the magic swirl around them once again and then come to wrap itself around me, and so I knew the spell had worked.

All the same, I had to hope it would never be put to the test.

I hugged all the gathered witches and thanked them, and one by one, they went upstairs and back to their own homes. When my mother and I were alone again, she sent me a piercing look.

"Are you going to tell me what happened tonight?"

"I came over here and joined the circle," I said disingenuously.

Because she was my mother, she saw right through that comment. "You're practically glowing, Charity," she replied. "And I know it's not the spell, because you were like that when you arrived."

Great. When I'd refreshed my makeup, I'd thought I looked better than I should have, considering everything that had happened today, but I'd just chalked it up to good lighting and a fun new shade of lip gloss. I hadn't realized that Noah's kisses had obviously had quite an effect on me.

"I liked being with Noah," I said, figuring that was something of an admission, even if I had no plans to tell her how my evening with him had ended in a couple of kisses. "I was worried about Milo, of course, but I'm not going to lie and say it wasn't fun to spend some time with Noah."

"Hmm."

That was all my mother said, but the way her russet brows drew together told me she didn't completely believe my story.

However, it seemed she'd either decided I'd suffered enough today, or she didn't have enough information to continue asking questions. Whatever it was, she only said she was glad he'd helped me, and admonished me to continue being careful, even though I now had some extra witchy protection watching out for me.

"I will," I said. "I'm going straight home after this—I'm wiped out."

A quick hug, and then I was walking back to my car. After I pulled away from the curb, my phone beeped from inside my purse.

Had my mother forgotten to tell me something?

No, that was a text from Noah.

> I talked to Troy and Ashley. She
> said she'll look into Dave
> Michaels tomorrow and see what
> she finds out. I'll call you as soon
> as I know something.

Brief and to the point, but the message still warmed me nonetheless. It was almost ten o'clock, and Noah could have waited until the next morning to reach out. Instead, he'd made sure to get in touch and keep me updated, probably guessing I'd feel much better about the situation if I knew we were making some progress.

Since I was driving—and since I'd never gotten the hang of having Siri write out a text while I dictated—I had to wait until I was parked in my driveway to respond.

> That's great. Fingers crossed
> they find something. Thanks so
> much.

With that handled, I went inside the house and locked the door. Although my coven had wrapped a spell of protection around me—and even though I'd cast my own warding spells on the house—I couldn't help looking out the window, thinking I might see a dark figure lurking in the bushes, or maybe cross the street in the shadow of the boat Ray Davidson always kept parked in his driveway, even though doing so was against local ordinances.

I didn't see anything, though, and told myself I needed to stop jumping at shadows.

No, I needed to get straight to bed, since I didn't know what the next day might hold.

Even though he'd only stayed with me a few days, it still felt strange to go downstairs the next morning and realize there was no Milo to feed, no need to let the dog out into the backyard so he could explore the new smells that had appeared since the last time he'd been outside. No doggy watching me as I made a plate of eggs, or begging for a bite of bacon.

Having him gone made me realize how much I'd loved having him around.

You're going to get him back, I told myself, but I wasn't sure I truly believed those words. Yes, Noah's detective friend was on the case, and my coven's spells should make sure the dog stayed safe no matter what Dave Michaels' nefarious plans for him might be, but neither of those things meant we'd actually be able to locate him and bring him home.

Since there wasn't much else I could do, though, I went ahead and got ready for work, then drove into town. Traffic was heavier today, telling me the crowds had already started to arrive this

Thursday morning in anticipation of the upcoming holiday weekend.

In a way, that was good. Enough customers came and went that I didn't have too much time to brood about Milo, although several people commented on the flyer I had posted on the bulletin board near the front door, saying they'd be sure to keep an eye out for the dog. Each of those well-meaning comments was enough to send a sharp little ping of worry through me, although I knew that hadn't been the intention of the people making them.

But it wasn't enough to keep me from focusing on the work, and Sage, correctly gauging my mood, didn't say anything about Milo. In fact, although I got the distinct impression she wanted to ask me about Noah Jenkins, she also avoided mentioning the vet or the way I'd spent hours with him the previous day putting up flyers. No, she was her usual cheery self, waiting on customers, answering questions, running out for a couple of burritos when it became obvious neither one of us would be able to take a real lunch break that day.

Around three, though, I got another text from Noah.

> Got some info. Can you meet me
> at my place at six?

Of course I could. I answered in the affirmative, and asked if I needed to bring anything.

> No, I figured we could order
> pizza, if that's okay.

I could have eaten pizza pretty much every day if I'd allowed myself to be so indulgent, and told him so.

He sent a smile emoji, followed by,

> See you at six. 2 Fairfield Street.

> See you then.

Well, it looked like my evening was taken care of. I found myself wondering why Noah hadn't just texted the information his private detective friend had dug up, then guessed he simply didn't have the time. His clinic was always busy, so he'd probably taken as much of a break as he could afford just to send me those quick texts.

Besides, it sounded like he wanted to see me in person, and who was I to argue with that?

I couldn't say the rest of the afternoon exactly flew by, but soon enough, Sage was locking the front door to the shop while I emptied the cash register. Since I wouldn't be meeting Noah until six, that gave me enough time to stop by the bank and drop off that day's cash. The credit card receipts went into a safe we kept on the premises, but I didn't like keeping cash around and always tried to deposit it as quickly as I could.

Sage and I said our goodbyes around five-thirty, and I scooted over to North Shore Bank to make my deposit. It felt as though half the population of Salem was in there that particular afternoon, but eventually I made it out at about five minutes until six.

That meant I was five minutes late making it over to Noah's house, but he didn't seem too worried about it. "Did you find the place all right?" he asked as he let me inside.

"Sure," I said. "I've lived here all my life. My best friend in sixth grade used to live just two doors down."

He sent me a rueful smile. "Right. I suppose I should've thought of that. Well, come on in. Sorry about the mess."

"Mess" was right. Or at least, his house was a lot more cluttered than I would ever have allowed my own place to be. Stacks of books sat on both the coffee table and the dining room table, which was also littered with piles of paper, some in folders, some not.

But I told myself it was just clutter, and not really dirty. It wasn't as though he had half-eaten sandwiches sitting on plates on the floor or anything like that.

"It's fine," I said.

He lifted an eyebrow, telling me he didn't really believe my reassurances, even if he wasn't going to come right out and say so. But then he shrugged and said, "I keep telling myself I need to stop working half-days on Saturdays, but there are enough people who can't make it to the clinic at any other time that I keep putting it off."

"Maybe you should hire a cleaning crew," I suggested, and he grinned.

"But I'd have to tidy up first before they could do anything."

About all I could do was smile in response to his comment. He went over to the coffee table and lifted the stacks of books out of the way, although all he did was set them on the floor on either side of the couch rather than returning them to the built-in bookshelves that flanked the fireplace.

Despite the clutter, the house was charming, obviously built in the late 1800s or thereabouts, with warm wood floors and lots of interesting details, like the stained glass transom window above the doorway that separated the living area from the dining room. I could see why he'd bought the place, especially since it was located only about five minutes away from his pet clinic. Even if he had to work crazy hours sometimes, at least he didn't have much of a commute.

"Some wine?" he asked next.

I'd learned my lesson about refusing a drink. "Sounds great."

He disappeared into the kitchen—I decided it was better to stay behind in the living room, just in case the sink was full of dirty dishes or something —and came back out a minute later holding one of those straw-wrapped bottles of chianti and a couple of wine glasses.

"I know it's kind of cheesy," he said as he set the glasses down on the coffee table and then pulled a corkscrew out of his back pocket. "But I always liked these bottles. And I figured chianti would be good with pizza."

"I love chianti," I told him. "And I like those bottles, too. I have quite the collection in my basement—I use them for candleholders when I'm sitting out on the patio."

"Then you can have this one when we're done with it."

Did that mean he expected us to drink the whole bottle tonight? Not that I minded too much, but I couldn't forget how we both had to get up and go to work in the morning.

"Great," I said.

He poured some wine for both of us, then indicated that I should go ahead and sit on the couch. Once I was settled, he sat as well, telling me, "We can order the pizza in a couple of minutes, but I figured I should go ahead and tell you what Ashley found out about David Michaels."

"Is that his real name?" I asked. All my instincts were telling me it wasn't, but I wanted to know for sure.

Noah shook his head. "No. The guy's name is Brian Alatorre. He's from Saint Louis, Missouri."

Alatorre? The man hadn't looked Hispanic to me, although I reminded myself that people's surnames weren't always a very good indicator of their appearance.

"So, what does he have to do with Darla Fitzgerald?"

"Nothing that Ashley could tell. But she also said that doesn't mean a lot, since she just got started with her investigation. Anyway, he's forty-one and single. Born in a suburb of Saint Louis called Richmond Heights, although he's lived in the city proper for the past fifteen years or so."

Saint Louis was far enough from Chicago that I still couldn't figure out why Brian Alatorre's and Darla Fitzgerald's paths would have ever crossed. They were around the same age, and right now, that was the only thing they seemed to have in common.

A sudden thought struck me. "Did Brian go to Northwestern, too?"

"No. Danielle said he went to a place called Washington University."

Well, there went that theory. Still, there had to be some kind of connection between the two, something we were missing.

I reached for my wine. Noah obviously also thought that was a good idea, because he lifted his as well. We didn't clink glasses, although we both sort of nodded at each other before we took our first sip.

"Ashley didn't find anything at all connecting the two of them?" I asked, even as I fought an over-whelming sense of futility. If the P.I. actually had discovered anything of real significance, I had to believe Noah would have mentioned it up front.

"Not so far," he replied. "But, like I said, she's just starting to dig into his past. She did say he's renting a condo near downtown, and she's going to try asking around to find out if anyone has seen Milo there."

A condo. I hated the idea of the dog being cooped up someplace with nowhere to run or even just go outside when he felt like it, even though I reminded myself that plenty of dog owners lived in condos and apartments and took care of their pets just fine.

We weren't talking about a dog owner here, though, but someone who'd taken Milo for reasons we had yet to discover.

"I doubt Mr. Alatorre would have done anything that careless," I said, and Noah let out a breath, as though to acknowledge the sad fact that our adversary, wily as he was, would have taken every precaution to make sure he couldn't be connected to the stolen dog.

"Probably not. But it's way too soon to give up. We just need to give Ashley more time."

Time. I could feel it ticking away, even as we sat here drinking wine. But what else could we do? I'd tried magic to track down Brian Alatorre, and so far it hadn't done me much good, except to provide the tiniest bits of information that Noah's friend had used to discover the man's real name and where he lived.

Well, that was something. I had to wonder what Mr. Alatorre would do if I suddenly turned up on his doorstep.

Not that I planned to do anything so reckless. No, I didn't have any real proof, only a bunch of circumstantial evidence that probably would never hold up in court, but I knew in my bones that he'd killed Darla Fitzgerald. I still didn't know the reason why, though, and confronting him without bringing along some backup in the form of the local SWAT team or something equally intimidating didn't seem like a very good idea.

"I know," I said, and stopped there, since I couldn't really think of what else to say.

Noah's expression was all sympathy. "I get it—it's hard. No one likes feeling helpless."

"You feel helpless sometimes?" I asked. He certainly wasn't arrogant, and yet he seemed so self-assured, so relaxed no matter what the situation, that I had a hard time imagining him feeling powerless.

"Of course I do," he replied without a single second of hesitation. "I feel that way every time someone brings in their old dog or cat, a pet who's been with them for fifteen years or more, and they beg me with their eyes to just give them another year or month or even a few days, but I know the only thing left is to give their pet as peaceful a transition as possible. Or when an animal is suffering, and again I know there isn't a surgery I can perform or a medication I can prescribe that's going to make a damn bit of difference. That's feeling helpless."

For a moment, I could only gaze back at him. This was definitely a side of Noah Jenkins I hadn't seen before, and I could only be grateful to him for letting me witness this moment of vulnerability.

"But you do what you can anyway," I said softly, and he nodded.

"Exactly. And that's what you have to do now, no matter how hard it might seem."

Again, I was silent, not sure of the best way to respond. He was right, of course—not knowing what was happening to Milo right now seemed almost unbearable, but I had to endure it for his sake. I had to be ready to take action when the time was right, no matter how beaten down I might be feeling right now.

"I will," I said steadily, and summoned a smile from somewhere. "So, let's go ahead and order that pizza."

Chapter 12

Heart of the Matter

WE SHARED OUR PIZZA, DRANK MOST OF the bottle of chianti, and kissed again at the end of the evening. On the drive home, I felt about a hundred percent better than I had before spending that time with Noah, but I still couldn't rid myself of the nagging feeling that I should be doing more.

I just had no idea what.

But after I'd drunk a glass of water and gotten ready for bed, it suddenly occurred to me.

Magic had helped me before, and maybe it could help me again. I'd been feeling stymied because so much of this kind of spell was centered on knowing who its object was, and using it to find "David Michaels" wouldn't have helped me at all. But now I knew his real name was Brian Alatorre, and that made all the difference in the world.

I kicked off the covers and stood, then grabbed

the light robe I always kept hanging from a hook in the master bath and went downstairs. There wasn't any hard and fast rule that I couldn't cast this kind of spell in my bedroom, but since I did almost all my magical work in the kitchen, it just seemed smarter to head down there to give myself the greatest chance of success.

In my cupboard I kept a special kind of elixir that I didn't sell in the shop, one I'd concocted specifically to make me as hyper-focused as possible when performing any kind of high-level enchantment. I got it out now, measured out a careful spoonful, and then swallowed. It tasted sweet, of honey and cinnamon and a hint of lemongrass, and, I hoped, would do the trick now.

While I had no doubt that Ashley would eventually dig up more useful information, I didn't want to rely solely on her to gather all that data. And now that I knew Brian Alatorre's real name, I had something I could actually use.

Some witches were adamantly against this kind of spell, saying it wasn't much more than magically fueled spying, and I actually did agree with them... on principle. But because the focus of tonight's spell was someone who'd probably killed Darla Fitzgerald and definitely had taken Milo, I wasn't going to scruple over digging into his private life through any means necessary. No, I needed to find out where the dog was and maybe—if I was lucky

—also learn exactly what the connection between Brian and Darla even was.

I poured some moon water into the silver bowl I always used for scrying, and set it down on the kitchen table. A few candles, a sprinkle of rock salt, and then I was ready to go.

Brian Alatorre
Tell me your story
Captured canine
Mine to find!

Maybe not the most elegant rhyme in the world, but the important thing was the magic that powered it and the object it was focused on.

The surface of the water rippled slightly, reminding me of a still pond touched by the smallest of breezes. Then it went quiet again, clear and empty.

I wanted to raise an eyebrow but quelled the impulse. Sometimes the images came quickly, while others took a minute or two to surface.

That seemed to be the case here, because after the water rippled again, I saw what looked like a small room in a motel, or maybe a very dingy vacation rental. Brian Alatorre sat on one of the two queen beds in the room, both of which were covered in a truly obnoxious rust and orange floral print that looked like it was right out of the 1970s.

Milo lay at the foot of the other bed, snout between his paws in a dejected posture I'd seen on more than one occasion. However, even though he looked far from cheerful, as far as I was able to tell, he seemed whole and healthy. In fact, just past him on the stained carpet was a set of plastic bowls, filled with what I assumed were food and water. The angle at which I was viewing the scene wouldn't allow me to see inside those bowls, but I didn't know what else could be in them.

As for Brian, he held his phone in his hands, although I also couldn't see the screen, so I didn't know whether he was scrolling through Facebook, watching a TikTok video, or reading his email. Whatever he was doing, he didn't look very happy.

The scene faded after that, and I frowned. While the scrying mirror had shown me Milo was fine, it hadn't given me a single clue that would let me know where the motel they were staying in was actually located. There had to be countless similar places scattered across the country, out-of-the way spots that didn't charge enough for their rooms to worry about updating the decor.

Although I wanted to be reassured, I didn't know whether I was. Brian had looked both angry and irritated, and I didn't think either of those emotions boded very well for the dog. For all I knew, he'd tried to dispose of Milo and hadn't been able to because of the protection spell that kept him swathed in a cocoon of negativity-warding magic. And yes, I supposed I could get the coven to keep renewing the spell as necessary, but this state of affairs couldn't continue indefinitely.

It looked like it was time to try again.

Brian Alatorre
Show me your story
How were you driven
To be so unforgiven?

Once again, the surface of the water rippled, but this time it went quiet immediately afterward, and then shimmered with a different image. This one showed Brian arguing with an older couple I guessed were probably his parents. Unlike him, they seemed as though they were definitely of Hispanic descent, both of them much darker than their son, handsome and friendly-looking.

Or at least, they felt like the sort of people who usually wore a pleasant expression on their faces, only now, the woman was clearly upset and the man obviously worried.

Brian was holding a piece of paper in his hand, and he shoved it toward the woman. She backed away, but her husband took the paper, looked down at it, and then shook his head, handsome features now sorrowful. He said something in response to what he saw on the piece of paper, but because the mirror only transmitted images, not sound, I couldn't understand what he was saying.

Maybe it was time to learn how to lip-read.

That wouldn't help me now, though.

What was on that piece of paper? What was so important that Brian had seen the need to confront his parents like this?

The image faded, so I didn't know what happened next. Clearly, he was upset about something.

Well, I'd just have to keep trying and see if the secret would give itself up to me. Normally, I wouldn't make so many attempts at scrying in a single evening, but there was absolutely nothing normal about these circumstances.

Brian Alatorre
Tell me your story
Secrets concealed
All now revealed.

It was like the water blinked. No ripples, no sign that it was going to do anything, but suddenly, I saw the paper, clutched in a pair of lightly tanned hands that I guessed must be Brian's, so different from his parents' warm brown skin.

It showed a multicolored bar graph and then a map with corresponding colors, and had 23andMe's logo at the top. A quick scan of the graph told me Brian Alatorre was mostly Irish and English, with a little bit of Scottish and German mixed in.

Absolutely nothing from Spain, or Mexico, or anywhere in Central or South America.

No wonder he was upset. I hadn't been able to hear what he was saying to his parents, but it sure looked to me as though he'd just discovered he was adopted. Why his parents had hidden such a thing from him—and why he'd believed them when they'd told him he was their biological son—I had absolutely no idea, but the situation had suddenly gotten a lot more complicated.

I didn't want to sympathize with him, but I could kind of understand why he'd be angry. However, the image still hadn't told me what all this had to do with Darla Fitzgerald...or with Milo.

When I tried to use the scrying mirror for a fourth time to get some more information, it remained stubbornly blank, letting me know that it had reached its limit for the evening.

Still, I'd learned a few things. Milo was safe, and something in Brian Alatorre's past seemed to be connected to this current mess, even if I couldn't figure out what that might be.

Well, I'd try to bounce some ideas off Sage in the morning and see if she had any insights she could offer. Sometimes all a problem needed was a fresh set of eyes looking at it, and I knew I couldn't reach out to Noah to let him know what I'd seen. Doing so would involve telling him about the spells I'd cast to peek into Brian Alatorre's life, and that was out of the question.

I thanked the mirror for its service, then opened the back door so I could go out into the garden and pour the moon water over some of my herbs. At other times of year, I used it to water my houseplants, but I liked to give the gift of the charged water to my herb garden when I could. The breeze off the ocean was cool but pleasant, and I breathed in the tang of salt.

Milo was safe for now.

I had to be content with that.

The next morning, I told Sage about what I'd seen in the mirror, and she frowned. "That's kind of crazy," she said. "But I'm glad Milo is okay."

For now, I thought, although I didn't utter those pessimistic words out loud. "I guess I'm just trying to figure out what possible connection Brian Alatorre could have to Darla."

Sage tilted her head, considering. We only had a few minutes until opening, after which I knew we wouldn't have a chance to talk, not on the Friday of Memorial Day weekend, when I knew the shop would be crazy busy. "Maybe they're related?"

I stared back at her. True, Brian and Darla resembled each other a lot more than he resembled his parents, but…. "How would he even know if they were?"

In answer, I got a smile that was almost but not quite condescending. "Oh, a friend of mine in high school did 23andMe because she wanted to learn more about her family background. She found a whole bunch of cousins in North Carolina she didn't even know about, and I guess what happened with her is that once you're in their database, it'll offer to show you connections to relatives."

"So you think Brian finally got suspicious about his heritage, took the test, and found out he was related to Darla Fitzgerald?"

Sage shrugged, then reached into the drawer where we kept the keys to the front door. "It makes about as much sense as anything else, doesn't it?"

I couldn't really argue with that observation. But even if it turned out that Brian and Darla were long-lost cousins or something, why would he have killed her? One would think he'd want to do whatever he could to get close to someone from his biological family, not put a bullet through her.

More questions, and definitely still not enough answers.

Because I knew there was no way I'd get a chance to take a long lunch today and maybe go see

Noah, I sent him a text as Sage headed over to the door to unlock it. There were already people waiting outside, so I had to make this fast.

> Can you have Ashley check to
> see whether Darla Fitzgerald ever
> took a 23andMe test? It might be
> important. Thanks!

The answer came back quickly—without, thank God, any probing questions.

> I'll have her look.

That was all, but it was enough for now. Maybe I was just a teeny bit disappointed that he hadn't asked about getting together for dinner, but I told myself seeing each other three nights in a row might have been a little much for a relationship that was just getting itself off the ground.

If what we had was a relationship at all. We still hadn't had what anyone could call a formal date.

That was fine, though. I'd rather have those evenings we'd shared than all the fancy dinners in the world.

For now, though, I'd have to put the mystery out of my mind and keep up with what I knew would be a pretty constant flow of customers.

Who knows...maybe I'd even be successful.

We were definitely so overwhelmed that neither Sage nor I had a chance to escape to grab some food. No, I had to quickly call in a Door Dash order and pray we'd be able to get through the next couple of days without falling over from exhaustion. Normally, Full Moon Apothecary was closed on Sundays and Mondays, but shutting down over a long weekend meant leaving a lot of money on the table, so I'd compromised by staying open on Sunday and giving both of us Monday off.

Noah texted me a little after four to say Ashley had confirmed that Darla Fitzgerald in fact had taken a 23andMe test about two years ago, and had bought the test as part of a group package she'd gotten for everyone at her PR firm as an offbeat sort of Christmas present. It actually made more sense she'd done it for that reason, because one thing witches did was closely watch their genealogy, making sure that even the girls without magic who were raised by relatives knew who they were and where they'd come from. At least we didn't have to worry about keeping track of boys, because the last thing anyone would have wanted was for some young witch to fall in love with her long-lost brother.

Her brother....

But witches didn't have brothers...did they?

As I'd thought a few days earlier, just because something had never happened before didn't mean it never would.

The thought that went through my head in that moment was too awful to contemplate, but I had to give it some space anyway.

Was it possible that Brian Alatorre and Darla Fitzgerald had been romantically involved, and he'd murdered her once he found out they were related?

That theory seemed a little more plausible, but it still didn't explain why he would have traveled all the way to Massachusetts to kidnap Milo. One would think that Brian would do everything he could to hide any possible connection he had to the woman he'd killed.

I didn't have time to ponder the conundrum further, because a tour bus disgorged its passengers right in front of the shop, and for a while, things were so squeezed I barely had time to breathe, let alone entertain any more thoughts on the subject of Brian Alatorre and Darla Fitzgerald.

When Sage finally locked the doors at a quarter after five and we were left mercifully alone, I discovered I'd missed a text from Noah.

> Are you up for some takeout tonight? I could swing by Thai Taste and grab some.

God bless Noah Jenkins, I thought. I definitely

wanted to see him, but at the same time, I didn't think I had enough brain cells to pick a place to eat.

> Sounds great. I should be home
> a little before six.

> I'll be there at six-thirty.

> See you then!

I put away my phone to see Sage smiling a little. "Was that Noah Jenkins?" she asked.

There didn't seem to be much point in hiding the exchange from her. "Yes. He's bringing over some takeout."

"You guys have been seeing each other a lot this week."

"And?" I asked, knowing the syllable sounded way too arch.

"And nothing," she responded, accompanying those words with a small lift of her shoulders. "He's a nice guy. I'm glad you've found somebody."

"I haven't 'found' anyone," I replied, although that protest sounded a little weak even to me.

"You've seen him every night this week," Sage said, obviously undeterred. "I think that qualifies. Anyway, see you tomorrow morning."

Before I could respond, she gave me a little

wave and headed out toward the back door. A moment later, I heard it bang shut.

That seemed to be my signal to go. Clearly, Sage had plans for this Friday evening, because her Nissan Leaf had already disappeared from the parking lot.

And I had plans, too. With any luck, I'd get home in just enough time to get myself fixed up so I wouldn't look quite as much like someone who'd been dodging tourists for the past seven hours.

Smiling, I backed out of my parking space and headed for home.

Was there anything more entrancing than the sight of a handsome man appearing on your doorstep with bags of Thai takeout in either hand?

Maybe there was, but if such a thing existed, I'd sure never seen it.

I welcomed Noah inside and guided him to the dining room, where I'd already set out some plates and had a bottle of rosé chilling in a painted ceramic holder. "I thought it would go well with the Thai food," I said, nodding toward the wine. "But if there's something else you'd rather have, just let me know."

"Rosé sounds great," he said. "Especially since

it was warmer today. It really does feel like the beginning of summer."

That was for sure, but mostly because of the holiday crowds that had thronged Essex Street today. We were definitely kicking off summer with a vengeance.

I dished up the food—spring rolls, brown rice, pad thai, cashew chicken—while Noah opened the bottle of rosé and poured some into each of our glasses. Once all that had been handled, he lifted his wine and gave me a speculative look.

"So...what prompted that question about 23andMe?"

Good thing I'd already thought of an answer, since I'd been pretty sure he was going to ask about that.

"It was something Sage said," I replied, which wasn't all that far from the truth. "It got me thinking about Brian Alatorre and how he definitely doesn't look Hispanic. If I were in that same situation, I'd probably start looking on my own if I didn't think I was getting the straight story from my parents."

Noah absorbed this information, expression thoughtful, and then he nodded. "So...that's why you asked whether Darla had ever taken the test? You think that's how she and Brian were connected, like long-lost relatives or something like that?"

"I know it sounds like kind of a reach," I allowed.

"Maybe not," he said. "I know I haven't come up with a better explanation for why the two of them would have known each other. But finding a relative you didn't know existed still doesn't seem like a good motive for murder. You'd think it would be his parents Brian was pissed at, not Darla Fitzgerald."

I'd thought pretty much the same thing, so I just shrugged and reached for a spring roll. "That's the part I don't understand, either. I keep thinking there's got to be a big piece of the puzzle we just haven't identified yet."

Noah helped himself to some pad thai, probably to give him some time to ruminate on what seemed to be an awfully tangled situation. "Ashley didn't have a lot more to tell me, either," he said after he'd swallowed the morsel. "Not beyond what I've already told you, that is. It sounds like the police are still investigating but don't have any leads yet, and it doesn't seem as if there was any physical evidence in the apartment, nothing to show Brian Alatorre was ever there. Her neighbors describe Darla as being almost relentlessly single."

If Darla Fitzgerald had gotten as much pressure from her family about procreating as I did from my mother, I could see why she'd take that stance. Deciding to go ahead and have children was sort of a leap of faith when you were a witch. The odds of having a child with talent were pretty good, but they weren't one hundred percent, and the consequences could be devastating when those wished-for magical gifts didn't appear.

"All those pictures on Darla's Facebook feed showed her and Brian out and about in public places away from her condo," I reminded him. "I have a feeling he worked hard to make sure no one who knew her would have seen them together. And I'm guessing she was just fine with that."

"But if no one saw them interacting, then trying to find a motive for her murder is going to be really hard," Noah replied. "It's not like the police even know where to look. You're the only one who has any idea the two of them might be connected somehow."

Right. For just a moment, I wondered if I should call the Chicago police department's tip line —I had to assume they had one—and leave them a message that they should look into a man named Brian Alatorre. Almost as quickly, though, I dismissed the idea. Sure, they could go talk to him, but I had to believe he'd stonewall any detectives who came his way, and with absolutely no evidence and not even an eyewitness who could claim to have seen them together, that part of the investigation would have hit an effective dead end.

Maybe I should stop playing good witch and

hurl a couple of curses his way. Unfortunately, I didn't practice that kind of magic, and even if I did, those curses wouldn't hit their target because I had no idea where the man actually was. Cursing wasn't the same as casting a spell of protection, like my coven had done for Milo. You absolutely needed to know where the object of a curse was so it wouldn't miss the person it was intended for and hit some innocent bystander.

Talk about your dead ends.

I didn't think I let out a sigh, but something in my expression must have told Noah how despondent I was feeling right then.

"Don't stress yourself out too much," he said with an encouraging smile. "Ashley's still working on it. Something has to give at some point."

"If you say so," I replied, and scooped up a forkful of cashew chicken. My appetite had deserted me, but I figured I'd better eat, if only to keep my strength up.

Some men might have pushed. Noah, on the other hand, only looked concerned but didn't say anything else. We ate in silence for a few minutes, and then he quietly poured a little more rosé into my glass.

"How about we go outside for a bit, if you're done eating?" he suggested.

That sounded like a great idea. "Sure," I said.

"Let's get the uneaten food packaged up first, though."

We closed up the containers the food had come in and then stored them in the refrigerator. That task done, we retrieved our wine glasses and headed outside. My house didn't have a deck, but the summer before, I'd had some pavers and a fire pit installed in an open space off to one side, and then set up a couple of outdoor sofas on either side of the fire pit. I didn't use it as much as I'd thought I would, although it was definitely the perfect destination for the two of us now.

Noah and I settled ourselves on one of the couches, glasses of rosé still in hand. The sun hadn't quite set, and a warm, golden light lingered on the garden. A sea breeze ruffled our hair, and insects hummed in the flowerbeds.

"You're right," I said. "This is much better."

"Yes, it is," he agreed. "Kind of amazing how a change of surroundings can help your outlook on life, isn't it?"

"That's for sure."

I sipped some of my rosé and breathed in the evening, the sights and scents and sounds around me, the utterly reassuring presence of the man who sat next to me on the couch. There was still so much I didn't know about him, mostly because we'd spent the majority of our time together discussing Milo's disappearance and the horrible crime it was connected to, but there was one thing I did know about Noah Jenkins.

I could trust him.

"We haven't talked much about ourselves," I said. "Is your family all in Boston?"

He smiled, obviously seeing right through my reasons for guiding the conversation in this direction. "Most of them," he said. "My parents and aunts and uncles and cousins. My little sister got married a couple of years ago and moved with her husband to Connecticut—New Haven. What about you?"

"I'm an only child," I replied. "So is my mother. I guess you could say our friends here are our real family."

A second or two passed before he asked quietly, "You never thought about leaving?"

Only about a million times, passed through my mind. Okay, that was possibly a slight exaggeration. When I was a teenager, though, I'd harbored plenty of fantasies about packing it up and going to school in New York and never looking back. Problem was, all the burden of being a witch would have been the same in the big city, except I wouldn't have had the same support system I did in Salem.

"Maybe once or twice," I said after a way too obvious pause. "But I love this town. Everyone I know is here, and I like that it's quiet and not too crazy."

"Except during holiday weekends," Noah joked, and I had to smile.

"And especially during Halloween," I added. "But it's still doable. I like being my own boss, too."

He nodded. "I get that. It's the same reason why I wanted to have my own practice here and not work for someone else."

Again, we fell quiet, but it was a comfortable kind of silence. Noah might have been wondering how someone my age could own her own house and business—especially when I knew lots of people who'd gone to college with me who were drowning in student debt and could barely afford a studio apartment—although he obviously was too polite to ask.

I could never tell him the truth, of course, that witches cast prosperity spells all the time—nothing crazy, but powerful enough to make sure we lived comfortable lives and never had to worry about paying the bills. Every once in a while, someone's wealth spell went a little off course, like the time Natalie Roberts' spell had her win more than a million dollars in the state lottery, but most of the time, it was all about making sure our investments did well for us or that we'd get an unexpected—but modest—windfall every once in a while.

And then Noah leaned over and kissed me, a kiss that was a little more passionate than the ones we'd previously shared. I responded in kind, feeling myself flush with need for him. At the same time, though, I knew I wasn't ready to go any further than this, not with Milo still missing and Brian Alatorre out there somewhere, plotting God only knows what.

Noah seemed to pick up on my reticence, or maybe he'd also realized this wasn't the place or time to have our relationship take the next step. "I never thought moving to Salem would get me embroiled in a mystery," he remarked, and the spell of the warm summer evening was broken.

"Oh, well," I said deprecatingly, "there's always some kind of craziness going on around here."

He chuckled. "I hadn't noticed."

That exchange seemed to be our signal that it was time for him to go. He didn't bother to head inside the house, but instead walked toward the gate in the side yard so he could go directly to the spot where his truck was parked on the street.

But once we reached the driveway, he paused and said, "Is there anything else I can do?"

"You've already done so much," I replied, even as I thought again what a treasure Noah Jenkins had turned out to be. "And honestly, this weekend is going to be so busy that I doubt I'm even going to have a spare moment to worry about what Brian Alatorre is doing."

A lifted eyebrow told me Noah didn't entirely believe my remark. However, he didn't press the issue, only said, "So busy that I can't take you out for a real dinner in a restaurant tomorrow night?"

"Well, maybe not *that* busy," I said with a smile. "Although I'm not sure whether you'll be able to get a reservation, considering the hordes will truly have descended by then."

His mouth quirked. "Well, let me worry about that. Pick you up at seven?"

"Absolutely," I replied without hesitation. No matter how tired I was going to be after a full day dealing with holiday weekend crowds, I wasn't about to turn down a really, truly actual date with Noah Jenkins.

A quick kiss goodnight—on the cheek this time, since we were standing out in full view of my neighbors, even though no one seemed to be outside—and then he made his way down the drive to his truck. I waved goodbye as he pulled away from the curb, and did my best to keep myself from grinning like an idiot.

I still might not have known where Milo was being held, but at least things seemed as though they were going swimmingly with Noah.

Chapter 13

Gone With the Wind

EVEN THOUGH I HAD BEEN FEELING MUCH more cheerful after I said goodbye to Noah, once I'd puttered around the house a little and tried to pick up the historical fiction tome I'd been reading before all this craziness intruded in my life, I realized I just couldn't concentrate. My mother would have said it was nothing more than my Virgo energy, always needing to be doing something useful, positively hating loose ends, but I thought it was more than that.

Spell or no, I was worried about Milo.

It seemed like the only person who would know anything about where Brian Alatorre might currently be was Darla Fitzgerald, but since she'd passed on from this plane of existence and I was just a witch and not a medium, there didn't seem to be much chance of me being able to talk to her.

But....

Where were her parents in all this? Obviously, Darla's mother was a witch, and therefore someone I could talk frankly to. Yes, Darla had been a grown woman and must have long since struck out on her own, but at the same time, witch families tended to stay close simply because of all the secrets we had to hide from the world.

Problem was, I had absolutely no real idea where the Fitzgeralds lived, except they were also in Chicago. Trying to locate a single household in a city that huge wasn't exactly an easy task.

Luckily, though, I had a solution to that particular conundrum.

No need for the scrying mirror this time, not when I was trying to unearth such a simple piece of information. Instead, I fixed the intention in my mind that I needed to have the Fitzgeralds' address, then chanted,

Whether near or far
Tell me where the Fitzgeralds are!

My phone pinged, and I startled. But when I went to retrieve it, thinking that maybe Noah had already gotten us dinner reservations and had sent me a message, instead I saw a few lines of text.

542 N. Hudson Street

Chicago, Illinois

Well, that made things easy. A quick piece of research told me the Fitzgeralds' house was located in an upscale neighborhood called Lincoln Park, not far from Lake Michigan.

But...now what? It was a little past eight-thirty, and since I wasn't a speedy broomstick rider like Stella Monroe, the trip would probably take me a little over two hours, which would put me at the Fitzgeralds' house close to eleven o'clock.

Not exactly a polite time to go calling at a stranger's home.

Except there was the time difference to factor in. If I left right now, I'd get to Chicago right before ten. Still not completely optimal, but better than my original estimate.

Which meant I needed to get my butt moving.

I didn't bother to tidy my hair or reapply my lip gloss, mostly because I knew the broomstick ride wouldn't help with my appearance anyway. Some witches—like Stella—could make their rides so perfect that their hair never got mussed and they didn't have to pick bugs out of their teeth, but I wasn't so lucky.

No, I just slung my purse over my shoulder, figuring I'd try to make any necessary repairs to my hair and face after I landed in Chicago, then grabbed my broomstick from its usual resting place near the hearth. Taking off from the backyard generally wasn't too risky, because I could shoot straight out over the cove and therefore away from my immediate neighbors' properties.

Still, I cast my usual "don't look at me" spell just to be safe, and did my best to ensure I flew with my mouth shut for those crucial first couple of minutes. After that, I was high enough to avoid any insect interference and could relax a little.

I didn't take these sorts of trips very often, and once about a half hour had gone by, I remembered why. Sure, to the layman, riding on a broomstick probably sounded as though it was lots of fun, but in reality, it wasn't all that comfortable. True, the same enchantment that kept me in the air sheltered me from the cold at that altitude, and I knew I wasn't in any danger of falling. All the same, it got pretty tedious after a while—if still better than having to stand in line at a TSA checkpoint—and I was very happy to start making my descent into Chicago around two hours after I'd left Salem.

Once again, I put the "don't look at me" spell in place, doing my best to make it extra-strong, since I would be landing in a strange location where I didn't know the territory at all. The ground rose up at me, thickly built with tall, narrow houses obviously designed to provide the most square footage on a small lot size, very different from the acre of lush gardens that surrounded my own home.

There was a lot more foot and car traffic than I'd expected, making me duck behind a nearby hedge so I could do my best to tidy my hair. The broom would have been horribly conspicuous, but I murmured a spell my mother had taught me when I was only ten years old, one that compacted my ride into a small hairbrush, something I could tuck in my purse until I needed it again.

A quick glance at my phone told me it was only a few minutes before ten o'clock, and I knew I couldn't waste any more time. I pulled in a breath, came out from behind the hedge, and then walked over to the neat brick path that cut through an equally tidy postage stamp of a lawn, and up a set of gray stone steps to the front door of the Fitzgeralds' house.

Once I was there, however, a sudden attack of the nerves assailed me. What if they weren't home? It was Friday night, after all. Or maybe they were home, but had guests over and wouldn't want to talk to me.

Almost at once, I dismissed that idea. Their daughter had been murdered only a few days earlier, so I sort of doubted they'd either be out partying or at home entertaining friends. Probably the worst thing I needed to worry about was whether they'd open the front door at all.

Well, I'd deal with that complication if and when it happened.

Before my courage could fail me again, I lifted my hand and pressed the small button next to the blue-painted front door. A simple "ding-dong" sounded somewhere inside the house.

It felt as though I waited there on the front stoop forever, but eventually, a fair-haired woman in her sixties with a thin, attractive face looked out at me. She resembled Darla more than I'd expected, telling me I'd definitely come to the right place.

But she was frowning, and I could tell she wasn't too thrilled about having an absolute stranger show up on her doorstep this late at night.

Time to talk fast.

"Mrs. Fitzgerald?" I asked, and she nodded.

"Yes, I'm Lara Fitzgerald."

Her tone was as dubious as her expression. "I'm Charity Hughes," I said. "I was watching Darla's dog Milo for her. Do you mind if we talk for a minute?"

As soon as I mentioned Milo, Lara Fitzgerald's expression shifted subtly. Maybe it was only that she knew I must be another witch, or Darla would never have left the dog with me. Now she looked more worried than skeptical, but at least she opened the door a little further, saying, "Of course, Ms. Hughes. Come inside."

From somewhere inside the depths of the

house I heard what sounded like a TV. A baseball game, I thought, since a burst of cheering drifted down the hallway, sounding oddly disembodied.

"My husband is watching the White Sox game," Lara said. "They're playing the Dodgers. So we can talk uninterrupted."

She led me to a room near the front of the house, obviously a parlor of some sort, with furniture that looked like real antiques and expensive oil paintings on the walls, which were a soft French blue. After we'd sat down on the white couch and I'd declined Lara Fitzgerald's offer of some tea, I thought I'd better start the conversation. Questions about Milo were probably inevitable, but I wanted to avoid them for as long as possible.

"I'm very sorry for your loss," I began, and Lara released a breath.

"It's been very difficult," she said. "I think the hardest part is not knowing exactly what happened."

Although I already knew the answer, I asked the question anyway, since it's what most people would have done. "The police don't have any leads?"

"Not really," she replied. "Nothing substantial, nothing that would lead me to believe they're going to solve the crime anytime soon."

"Maybe I can help with that," I said. "Do you

know anything about a man named Brian Alatorre?"

She shook her head, looking puzzled. "I don't think so. At least, I know I've never heard that name before."

"He's a man who knew your daughter," I said. "I don't know exactly what their relationship was, though. I saw them in some Facebook photos together."

Now Lara Fitzgerald appeared even more confused. "My daughter didn't waste time on social media," she said, sounding almost prim. "At least, not beyond what the work at her firm required."

Not the best opening, but I knew I needed to take it. "This might sound strange, but do you have any idea how the two of them might be related? Maybe through your husband's family? Because it's sounding more and more like Brian Alatorre found your daughter through 23andMe, one of those ancestry DNA sites."

At once, Lara went almost white. The lighting wasn't the best in the room where we sat, true, but still, I could practically see the way the blood drained from her face.

"It's not possible," she breathed, and I stared at her.

"What's not possible?"

In answer, she got up from the couch and went

over to the fireplace, which was as coldly formal as the rest of the room, with its white marble surround and angular plaster mantel. Sitting on that mantel were pictures of a much younger Darla, along with a blond man that I guessed must be her father.

When Lara turned back around, her mouth was set, almost grim. "I'm going to tell you this," she said, "only because I think this Brian Alatorre person could be the one responsible for my daughter's death, although I can't say exactly how or why. The thing is...."

The words trailed away, and I noticed how her fingers had clutched a fold of the linen skirt she was wearing, leaving an obvious crease. Whatever she was about to tell me, it couldn't be good.

I waited silently, somehow knowing that if I interrupted her, she might lose her nerve and wouldn't tell me what I so desperately needed to hear.

"Darla had a brother," Lara said softly. "A twin brother."

About all I could do was stare at her, my brain unwilling to process what she'd just told me. "That's impossible," I breathed.

Everyone knew that witches never had male children.

Her mouth twisted in grim amusement. "I thought that, too...until the moment my son was born. Luckily, I'd chosen to have my child at home, assisted by a witch who was also a midwife. Charles —my husband—never even knew he had a son. The midwife took the boy away, saying she would leave him where he could be placed with a mundie family."

The Alatorres, of course. About a million questions swirled around in my brain, but I blurted out the one that rose to the surface first.

"How could you give him up when you didn't know whether or not he would have any magical talent?"

She crossed her arms. "All witches are women. There was absolutely no way in the world the child would ever share our gifts. It was better to send him away someplace where he could be raised by people who would love him for who he was. Besides, how could I ever admit to the other members of my coven that I'd given birth to a boy?"

That last word came out of her mouth with roughly the same inflection as someone saying "cockroach." Obviously, she didn't want to be connected to such an aberration.

Anger at her selfishness flared in me, but I tamped it down as best I could. Lara Fitzgerald had made her decision while her body was awash in pregnancy hormones, and she probably hadn't been thinking straight.

"Can I talk to the midwife?" I asked.

"No. She passed away about five years ago."

So much for that idea. Still, the pieces of the story were starting to come together, even if I still couldn't figure out why Brian Alatorre would have seen the need to kill Darla Fitzgerald. One would have thought they'd be united in their anger against their mother, both for giving up the child she'd just acknowledged to me...and for keeping that secret from the rest of her family for all these years.

"You think he did it, too, don't you?" Lara said next, her tone as cold and steely as a knife that had been stored in a freezer.

I hesitated. "Maybe. I don't know. I'm still trying to figure out why in the world he'd do something so awful."

"How did you get involved in all this, anyway?" she asked. "You're the familiar-whisperer, right?"

The phrase wasn't my favorite, but so many people in the witch community referred to me that way, I'd long since given up trying to correct them. "Like I said, I was watching Milo," I replied.

Lara's expression hadn't softened in the slightest, even at my mention of the dog. "Yes, Darla said she was having trouble with him. He stopped speaking."

For a moment, I wondered if I should tell her that Milo's silence had been due to a spell Darla had cast and nothing more. It came to me then that

Darla had probably hexed her own familiar because it had given her an excuse to remove the dog from harm's way and make sure he'd be safe with me. I didn't get the chance to comment, though, because Lara Fitzgerald continued.

"That was something the two of us never agreed on," she said. "Darla struggled with being a witch, and even more so after she realized she was going to have a familiar with her for the rest of her life. She was not always kind to the dog, and I felt that was very unfair."

I honestly couldn't understand how anyone could be cruel to a creature as sweet and loving and friendly as Milo, but in the end, it might have been all for the best. "I think that's what saved him when she died," I said softly. "Otherwise, a strong connection would have taken him with her."

Lara Fitzgerald's eyes widened. "Milo is still alive?"

"Yes," I responded. Should I tell her more, or should I let it go? It seemed better to let her know exactly where I stood on the subject of Darla's former familiar. "He's going to have a home with me," I told Lara, tone firm enough that it didn't leave much room for argument.

Not that I could imagine Darla's mother with a dog running around her showcase of a home. Milo was very conscientious, but with dogs, there was always a chance of mishaps.

Because she relaxed visibly, I could tell Lara had been worried that I'd come here to tell her she needed to adopt her daughter's familiar. Now she wouldn't have to worry about the dog, could tell herself he was in exactly the right place for him.

"Anyway," I went on, "that's why I'm trying to find out what happened. And since it turns out that Brian Alatorre is from a witch family, it's probably better that I handle this rather than the authorities."

Alarm flickered again in her hazel eyes, so like Darla's...and Brian's. "Yes, that's much better," Lara said hastily. "It's important that none of this ever gets out. Do you understand?"

Oh, I sure did. She'd been sweeping her son's existence under the rug for forty-plus years and wanted to continue doing so. It didn't matter what happened to him, as long as her secrets never saw the light of day.

Well, I'd do my best. I was just a witch who brewed elixirs and tinctures and grew herbs, not James Bond or Dirty Harry. As soon as I had enough evidence to prove Brian's guilt, I was going to turn it over to the police and let them arrest the man.

However, that didn't mean I'd ever tell them anything about Brian Alatorre's true origins.

"The problem is," I said. "I don't know where to find him. He's out there somewhere—I glimpsed him in my scrying mirror once, but it didn't give me any details."

Lara frowned. It seemed obvious she wasn't happy about that revelation. "You need to track him down," she said, her voice flat.

Working on it, I thought, but didn't bother to say the words out loud. Even though I'd only just met her, I could tell she was the kind of person who wanted results, not excuses.

But then her expression cleared. "Maybe I can help. Wait here."

I stared at her nonplussed, but nodded anyway. Without saying anything else, she left the parlor and headed up the stairs, her heels clacking enough on the wooden treads that I was glad her husband had the TV turned up so loud. It still seemed a little odd to me that he hadn't come to see who had been at the door or what had been occupying his wife for the past fifteen minutes, but maybe she hadn't been watching the game with him, and so there was no reason for him to expect her back in that part of the house.

It seemed all too possible that he was buried in grief for his daughter, and the best thing he could think of to try to blank it out was to lose himself in whatever game might be on TV at any given time.

A few minutes later, Lara descended the stairs. In her hands, she carried a small white blanket, now yellowed with age along its edges.

"He was wrapped in this," she said, her voice hushed even though there was no way her husband could hear us over the blaring sound of the White Sox/Dodgers game. "Marelie took him away in something else, but she first wrapped him in this blanket after he was born. I washed it once and then hid it away. It might help you find him."

She handed the blanket to me, and I took it. No, I didn't get an instant flash of where Brian Alatorre was currently holed up, but she was right —the correct spell might allow me to use the blanket to track him down to his current hiding place.

Before I could thank her, she went on, "Just... whatever happens, I don't want to know. I only had one child, and she died four days ago."

So many things I wanted to say, none of which would have been right. I didn't know what I would have done in Lara Fitzgerald's place.

I didn't know much of anything, except that this interview had been even more painful than I'd imagined.

Still holding the blanket, I got up from the couch. I only said, "I'm sorry," then left the room and let myself out. Once I was back in the fresh air —or at least, as fresh as it could be in Chicago, which felt and smelled very different from Salem, Massachusetts—I sucked in a breath, then went back to the hedge that had hidden me before. I used its cover to restore my broomstick to its original shape and function, and took to the air again.

Now I just had to see whether the "help" Lara Fitzgerald had given me would actually be of any use.

Chapter 14

Wipe Out

It was going on 1 a.m., and I should have been in bed at least an hour earlier, considering how crazy it was going to be at the shop that Saturday.

Instead, I stood in my kitchen, Brian Alatorre's baby blanket spread out on the table, and considered my options.

The first one would be to wait until I could talk to my mother and Grace Bowersby and some of the other members of the coven to get their input. But I'd seen the shame in Lara Fitzgerald's face as she recounted what had happened on that fateful night so many decades ago, and I knew I didn't want to air her dirty laundry unless I absolutely had to.

The second was to decide which spell would be most likely to wake up the long-buried connection between Brian and the blanket I'd placed on my kitchen table, and then act on whatever information it provided.

The third—and the most cowardly—would be to say all this was way above my pay grade, and to just go into work the next morning as though nothing significant had happened the night before.

I couldn't do that to Milo, though. He was counting on me...mostly because, if our situations had been reversed, he wouldn't have hesitated to come to my aid.

Which is why I was standing there in my kitchen at one o'clock in the morning, mentally thumbing through all the various flavors of spells I knew and trying to decide which one would be the most useful in this particular situation. Some witches had a gift for psychometry—touching an object and picking up on the vibes it contained— but I wasn't one of them.

No, I'd have to do this the old-fashioned way.

I reached out and laid my hands on the blanket. Not to pick up its vibrations, though, but to make sure I had as much contact with it as possible.

Show me the son
Cast off, undone
Where he's hiding
Always abiding

A sharp tingle moved up both my arms. Startled, I almost let go of the blanket before I realized that doing so might interfere with the spell I'd just cast. Instead, I gripped it harder, willing the magic to show me what I needed to know.

Again I saw the image of that shabby motel room. This time, though, Brian Alatorre seemed to be asleep, head lolled back against the pillows he had propped up behind him. Milo, on the other hand, was awake, lying on the floor with his snout pointing toward the door, almost as though he was expecting someone, and I expelled a breath of relief.

Maybe that someone he waited for was me.

Hopefully soon, kiddo.

The image didn't remain static, though. Instead, the scene panned past, as though I was watching the whole thing on my TV screen, and moved outside, showing a panoramic shot of the motel. It was just about as rundown as I'd imagined, with faded paint and a few missing shingles on the roof.

However, it wasn't the condition of the building that really caught my attention. No, it was the neon sign that flashed tiredly from its post next to the road.

Sleepeasy Motel.

Maybe there was more than one motel with that name, but I kind of doubted it.

The spell apparently thought it had shown me everything it needed to, because the image blinked away, leaving me standing there, holding the blanket.

Well, that made things easier.

I grabbed my phone and hurriedly opened the Safari browser, then entered the words "Sleepeasy Motel." Several hits came up, telling me I'd been wrong in thinking the one the spell had shown me was unique.

However, one of those hotels was all the way out in Montana, while the other was just up the road in New Hampshire.

Guess which one Brian Alatorre was currently holed up in?

All right, I didn't know for sure, but I figured it must be the motel in New Hampshire. I still had no idea what he was planning, but it just made sense for him to have stayed relatively nearby. Also, since he couldn't ride a broomstick and had to travel like the normal human being he was, it would have taken him days to drive to Montana, and I honestly didn't think he would have wanted to be cooped up in a car with a dog for that long.

So, now I had a pretty good idea of where he was. The real trick would be figuring out what to do next.

My first thought was to contact the New Hampshire state police and let them know a dangerous fugitive was holed up at the Sleepeasy Motel. The problem with that particular plan, though, was that Brian Alatorre currently wasn't a person of interest with the Chicago P.D., and the New Hampshire authorities would probably dismiss my claims as bogus.

Or worse, if they actually did go to investigate, Brian might laugh the whole thing off and tell them I was a crazy ex-girlfriend who was just angry because he'd kept our dog after we broke up. Obviously, he was good at making himself convincing, probably even charming, or someone as usually brittle and standoffish as Darla Fitzgerald would never have even allowed him into her orbit.

Well, desperate times called for desperate measures. And I was a witch, and that meant I had more than a few tricks up my sleeve.

Time to make a solid plan.

Brian was asleep. My image had made it look as though he was pretty much down for the count, and what better time to go in and retrieve Milo without his captor even realizing that I'd dropped in to grab the dog?

A locked door couldn't keep a witch out—one simple spell would have that motel room open, pronto. Another spell would deepen Brian's sleep, ensuring that he'd snore right through me slipping in and getting Milo out of there. Once the two of us were safely back at my place, then I could call the police station nearest to the Sleepeasy Motel. Maybe they'd believe me and maybe they wouldn't, but I would have done what I could. I'd also contact the authorities in Chicago to let them know the murder suspect they were looking for was currently holed up in a cheap motel in New Hampshire.

And Milo would be back with me, and safe. I supposed there was always a chance Brian would try to kidnap him again, but now I knew who to look out for and wouldn't let my guard down for a second. With any luck, he'd realize he'd been thoroughly beaten and would slink back to Chicago.

Or Timbuktu, for all I cared. I just wanted him out of Milo's life...and mine.

I really wished I could have Noah along for backup, but I didn't dare put him in that kind of danger. Besides, this raid was going to require magic, and obviously, I couldn't use it around him without him asking questions I simply couldn't answer.

Not without giving away the entire witch community, that is.

The thought crossed my mind that it was absolutely crazy to be confronting someone I knew was a killer, alone and without any assistance. But Milo was my responsibility, and if I didn't want to put Noah in harm's way, I couldn't very well ask anyone else to come along.

Contacting the local authorities wouldn't do any good, because it would be Brian's word against mine.

Also, although I'd never had any need to use them, I had a couple of spells that were purely offensive in nature that I could throw at Brian Alatorre if I had to. I'd prefer to avoid that sort of thing, just because one misplaced fireball could burn down a whole building—not to mention attract all sorts of unwanted attention—but if I had to hurl lightning bolts at the guy to get Milo safely away, so be it.

I looked over at the clock on the stove.

Fifty minutes past midnight...still the witching hour.

Time to get going, even though every muscle and bone in my body was telling me it was way too late for this sort of thing, and I just needed to go to sleep and figure this out in the morning.

Well, that wasn't going to happen. The best time to go after Brian was when he was dead to the world, as my vision had shown, and that meant I needed to do this thing, no matter how tired I might be.

I glanced at my phone again to remind myself of the motel's address, then picked up my broomstick.

"Forty-two State Route 76," I told it, and did my best to quell the tremor of unease that went through me. I couldn't give in to my nerves right now.

I had a dog to save.

This time, we launched right from the back door, since I figured it was late enough that none of my neighbors would be out prowling around their gardens at this hour. Of course, I wasn't in such a rush that I still didn't cast my little "look over there" spell to conceal my departure. Taking that kind of precaution was something that had been ingrained in me from the time I was old enough to take my first broomstick ride.

Because I was going a much shorter distance, I'd barely reached altitude before I needed to make my descent toward the wooded property where the motel was located. I was glad so many trees clustered around the place, since that made it much easier to land in an inconspicuous spot.

Dead leaves crackled under my feet as I dismounted from my broom, but no one was near enough to notice. Some voices drifted toward me from the motel's parking lot and I froze, glad of the cover a clump of pine trees provided.

Then I heard an engine start up, and a pair of headlights flashed through the darkness before the vehicle turned onto the highway that fronted the motel and disappeared, heading north.

I let out a breath, even as I prayed that the departing car hadn't belonged to Brian Alatorre. It wasn't as though I couldn't give chase on my broomstick, but it would definitely ruin any chance I might have of sneaking up on him.

Still with the "look over there" spell protecting me—and with my broomstick compacted and stowed in my pocket—I emerged from the trees and made my way toward the motel's lobby. Like the rest of the place, it was dark, but that wasn't a problem.

Neither was the lock on the door. I hated to break in, but while my vision had showed me the Sleepeasy Motel, it hadn't revealed which unit Brian was sleeping in. The last thing I wanted was to burst into some unsuspecting tourist's room and scare them half out of their wits.

According to the old-fashioned paper ledger at the front desk...thank God the motel's management hadn't bothered to join the twenty-first century with the rest of us...four of the motel's seven units had been rented. Three of them had couple's names on them, but the fourth had been rented to someone named David Michaels.

Clearly, he hadn't bothered to come up with a different alias, or maybe he had fake identification under that name and figured he might as well keep on using it.

Not that it mattered. What really mattered was that I now knew he was staying in Room Number 7, at the far edge of the building.

In a way, that was a good thing. If I actually did have to launch a fireball or two, it was less likely the damage would spread to the rest of the motel than if he'd been staying in one of the units in the middle of the building.

I quietly exited the office and used another spell to re-lock the door. All of the windows were dark as I tiptoed past, telling me the people who'd rented those rooms were fast asleep, just like Brian Alatorre.

Good. If my luck held, I could be in and out of here long before anyone was awake enough to notice.

When I got to the door for Number 7, I paused outside for a moment, mentally taking my bearings and reminding myself of the room's layout. Not that there was a whole heck of a lot to remember— it had two queen beds with a single nightstand separating them, and a low dresser on the opposite wall that held an old-fashioned, blocky TV that probably dated from at least the 1990s, if not even earlier. No table by the window, no other furniture except one of those folding stands designed for holding a suitcase.

And Milo lying on the floor not far from the door, and Brian snoozing on the bed a few feet away. It would have been better if he'd been on the farther bed, closer to the bathroom, but I figured I should still be able to slip in and out without him noticing.

I placed my fingers on the doorknob and whispered the same spell I'd used to break into the motel's office. Immediately, I could feel the tumblers shift in the lock, even though they didn't make any sound. A pause to quickly recite a sleep spell directed at the man who slumbered inside the room, and then I turned the knob and opened the door.

Just as I'd seen in my vision, Milo was lying only a few feet away. He perked up at once as he caught sight of me, tail wagging furiously.

I put my finger to my lips, telling him he needed to stay quiet. Good thing he was a familiar and understood immediately, because in most other cases, he might have let out a bark of greeting, and that would have dashed any hopes of getting away without being noticed.

Even so, I sent a worried glance toward the bed where Brian slept. He hadn't moved, still lay there propped up against the pillows. It didn't look like a very comfortable position to me, but then a faint snore drifted out from his open mouth, telling me he remained very much asleep, and that my spell had obviously worked.

Let's go, I mouthed to Milo, and he got to his feet and began moving toward the door.

He was only a foot away when the light on the nightstand flicked on, and I froze.

Brian Alatorre was sitting up in bed, an extremely unpleasant smile on his lips.

"Going somewhere?"

Chapter 15

True Crime Confessions

BAD ENOUGH HE WAS AWAKE. WHY THE hell hadn't my sleep spell worked?

Much worse, though, was the ugly snub of a pistol's barrel poking out from underneath the covers, pointed straight at my head.

"Close the door and back away," he commanded.

Cursing mentally, I did as he said and then moved a few more feet into the room. Yes, I had the coven's protection spell supposedly guarding me from all harm, but right then, I wasn't sure whether I wanted to put it to the test, considering what the consequences might be if it failed.

Still, if I was stuck here for now, I planned to get as many answers as I could.

"Why did you kill your twin sister?" I asked.

That might have been grudging respect in his

expression. It was hard to say for sure, because the bedside lamp wasn't very bright, and cast odd shadows across his sharp features.

"How'd you figure that out?" he returned.

"Because I talked to Darla's mother," I said. "She confessed that she'd had twins and gave the boy up for adoption."

Brian's mouth twisted. "That's a nice way of putting it. More like threw me away like a piece of garbage."

"She said the midwife put you up for adoption."

Now he paused. "I was adopted, sure. A nice little black-market baby, one she probably got a huge price for."

"Did your parents tell you that?" Despite all the terrible things Brian had done, I couldn't help feeling just a bit sorry for the guy. It couldn't have been easy for him to learn his adoptive parents had lied to him his entire life.

His gaze slipped away from me for just a second. Not long enough for me to dive for the gun—not that I'd attempt anything so crazy when one slip of his finger on the trigger could put my protection spell to a sudden, violent test—but enough to tell me he wasn't comfortable talking about the people who'd given him a home and a name.

"They didn't want to talk about it," he said at

length. "Which, fine, whatever. But Darla—she talked plenty."

For the first time, Milo moved, coming over to take a protective stance in front of me. I wanted to shake my head, to tell him he shouldn't do anything foolhardy, but I also didn't want to signal that I was worried about the dog's safety. Brian Alatorre was way too much of a loose cannon for me to guess what he might do next.

"Talked about what?"

He tilted his head, that unpleasant smile still playing around his mouth. "About how she was a witch." A pause before he added, "Just like you are."

I didn't bother to ask how he knew that. From what I could tell, he knew a whole lot of things he wasn't supposed to.

"Sure," I said easily. "But why did you kill her? Why take the dog?"

Now Brian chuckled, although it was far from a friendly sound. "You ask a lot of questions."

"I do," I replied. "You got the drop on me, so yes, I guess you don't need to tell me anything. But you kind of want to, don't you?"

He didn't answer right away. Instead, he pushed back the covers, showing that he wore a blue T-shirt and a pair of beige cargo shorts, and looked like a typical guy off traveling on Memorial Day weekend.

Well, not completely typical, considering that both his forearms were swathed in bandages. Beneath those wrappings, I guessed, were the wounds Milo had given him during the attack. No wonder the man had fled the scene so quickly. It hadn't been a reluctance to go after the dog that had made him run away, but the simple need to get out of there before he lost too much blood.

A slight push, and he was standing upright, the barrel of the pistol still pointed directly at me.

"Darla didn't much like being a witch," he said. "I didn't really understand that, because who wouldn't want to have those kinds of powers? But she just wanted to be normal, and when she realized we were actually brother and sister, she was glad, because she thought I was normal and wanted to be like me."

"'Thought' you were normal?" I repeated, not sure I liked the sound of that. "Does that mean you're not?"

"Oh, I'm just a regular guy," Brian replied easily. "But that doesn't mean I don't have ambitions. And this whole witchy thing could have been really profitable."

Maybe so. He could have asked Darla to cast some prosperity spells for him, asked her to find him a winning lottery ticket, whatever.

I said as much, and he just smiled again, this time a condescending lift of his mouth that seemed to indicate he didn't think much of my imagination.

"She did at first," he said. "But then when she told me she was on the Witch Olympics committee and had visual proof of witches showing off their powers, that's when I started to realize she was sitting on a goldmine."

"How do you mean?" I asked, even as I experienced a sinking feeling somewhere in my gut. One of the first things a witch learned was to never, ever let outsiders know anything about her powers, but if Darla had decided to abandon those rules in her need to connect with her long-lost twin brother....

Once again, Brian sent me one of those singularly condescending stares. "You can't really be that dense, can you?" Without waiting for me to respond—not that there was any way to politely reply to such an insulting question—he went on, "She had recordings of witches flying broomsticks, throwing lightning bolts, making things turn invisible. We could have sold that stuff to the highest bidder and made millions."

"I don't know about that," I told him, glad I at least sounded dubious and not completely scared out of my wits, both for myself and the entire witch community. "CGI and stuff like that is so good these days, a lot of people would think those videos were faked."

Judging by the scowl which creased his forehead after I delivered my remark, it seemed pretty obvious Brian Alatorre wasn't very happy with me at the moment. "But they weren't faked," he said, his tone way too taut. "And they would have stood up to all sorts of scrutiny. In fact, I would have welcomed it, because that would have been a way to get experts to certify the contents of the videos were real."

I still wasn't so sure. On the other hand, I didn't think it was a very good idea to keep arguing with a man who was pointing a gun at me.

"So, you were going to sell the videos," I said. "What happened?"

His scowl only deepened. "Darla changed her mind," he replied. "Said that just because she didn't like being a witch, it didn't mean she could betray the rest of her sisters. Sisters," he repeated, tone dripping with contempt. "Like she was related to any of the rest of you. The only relation she had was me."

"And you killed her," I said.

He shrugged. "We made a deal, and she tried to back out of it. She wouldn't give me the videos when I asked for them. So...that was the end of it."

Apparently. He hadn't described exactly what had happened, but he didn't need to. Angry about Darla's betrayal, he'd gone to her condo and shot her.

"But why the dog?" I asked next, and Milo's

tail wagged uncertainly. He was still taking his cues from me, and the longer I could keep Brian talking, the more chance I had of figuring out how to get the two of us safely out of here. Not for the first time, I wished I could just snap my fingers and wish myself someplace far, far away, but that wasn't how my powers worked. There were some witches who could manage teleportation, but they were few and far between.

Unfortunately, the only way I was getting out of this room was on my own two feet.

Brian's eyes narrowed, and I got the feeling he wasn't a fan of Milo any more than Darla had been.

Poor dog.

"He was her companion," Brian said. "He knew everything...including where she had those videos hidden. I figured I'd grab him and make him talk."

"That's not how it works," I said. "Darla could talk to Milo because he was her familiar. No one else—not a regular person, not another witch—can understand what he's saying."

"But *you* can, can't you?" Brian returned, his tone now turning soft, almost insinuating. "I saw it on her phone after I killed her. A calendar entry for dropping Milo off with the 'familiar whisperer,' along with your address."

Thanks, Darla, I thought. So that was how Brian had even known where to find the dog. She was probably one of those people who kept everything on her phone, figuring its security features would be enough to prevent anyone from gaining access to such confidential information.

Of course, that begged the question of how Brian had been able to get past that same security.

I probably didn't want to know the answer, but I asked anyway. "And how were you able to see what was on Darla's phone?"

A shrug that was chilling in its utter unconcern. "She had it locked down with that Face ID thing. I just held the phone in front of her face—it couldn't tell she was dead."

Cold ran down my spine. I didn't know what was worse—Darla's iPhone not being able to recognize that the face it was seeing was dead, or Brian coldly using the visage of the woman he'd just killed to break into her phone.

"Anyway," he went on, still in that horribly nonchalant tone, "it's good that you're here, actually. Saves me another trip to Salem. Ask the dog where Darla hid those videos."

I absolutely hated how Brian said "the dog," as though Milo wasn't an individual with his own thoughts and fears and needs. And there was absolutely no way I'd ever give that information to Darla's killer, especially now that I knew what he planned to do with it.

My own safety didn't matter much compared

to all the lives that would be disrupted if that information got out.

"No," I said.

Surprisingly, Brian didn't seem too worried by my flat refusal. He came closer, and pointed the gun at my knee. "Blowing out your kneecap won't kill you," he told me, still sounding utterly casual. "But it'll hurt a lot. Does being a witch give you a higher tolerance to pain?"

Of course it didn't. Witches were just regular human beings with a few special abilities.

But I lifted my chin and said, "What do I get out of it if I help you?"

He cocked an eyebrow at me, clearly surprised by the question. "Besides getting to continue breathing?"

"Yes, besides that," I said coolly. I didn't trust him any further than I could throw him, but it still seemed smart to keep Brian Alatorre talking for as long as possible. Next to me, Milo tilted his head, as if he, too, couldn't quite understand where I was going with this.

Unfortunately, I'd just have to hope he trusted me enough to go along with whatever I did or said.

Since Brian was still looking a little confused, I added, "You're asking me to help you reveal a secret that's been hidden for generations. Witches have died to make sure no one ever knew the truth about us." *Including Darla Fitzgerald,* I thought with an inner shiver. "So...what's in it for me?" I asked.

"Ten percent," he said immediately. "And getting to stay alive."

He probably thought he was being generous.

Pretending to play along, I countered, "Fifteen percent."

A long pause while he stood there, staring at me. The gun was still pointed at my knee, and I found myself wondering almost absently how much it would actually hurt to get shot in the kneecap.

A lot, probably.

Then Brian surprised me by saying, "Okay... fifteen percent. But you need to get the dog to tell you where Darla put all those recordings."

Crunch time. I had to make it look as though I was cooperating and doing my best to get Milo to provide that much-needed piece of information, but without actually divulging anything of any real importance.

Luckily for me—and the rest of the witch world by extension—Brian wouldn't be able to understand a thing Milo said to me in response to my questions, which meant I could twist this any way I needed to.

Thank God for small favors.

Without directly responding to Brian's demand, I turned to the dog. His tail wagged again, although still in that half-hearted sort of way, telling me he knew we were in a world of trouble even if he hoped I'd be able to find a way out of all this.

You and me both, buddy, I thought.

"Milo, where did Darla hide those videos?"

A head tilt, and Milo replied, "She was worried about that man doing something with them, so she took them away and hid them."

Standing a few feet away, Brian watched this exchange with some suspicion, but seemed ready to wait and see what happened.

For now, anyway.

"Do you know where?" I asked, wondering what the heck I would do if it turned out Milo didn't know the answer to my question.

But his nose wrinkled a little, and he said, "She put them in a box and took them to her mom's house."

That piece of information startled me. True, I still didn't have a very good grasp of exactly what Darla's relationship with her mother had been like, but I also hadn't thought she would have trusted Lara Fitzgerald enough to keep something so important...and possibly incriminating...at the home where she'd grown up.

On the other hand, her house in Lincoln Park was the sort of place where most people wouldn't think to look. Also, even though I hadn't seen evidence of one, I guessed the home had some kind of security system, thanks to all the expensive art and antiques it contained.

I looked back over at Brian, whose eyes were still slightly narrowed. Clearly, I needed to make this good, or he'd never believe me.

Mixing some truth in with the lies, I said, "Milo saw her box up the videos and take them away."

"Does he know where she took them?"

"He says he rode with her to a place that had a lot of little buildings. I think he was trying to describe a storage facility."

A beetle-browed glance at the dog, and then back over to me. "Which storage facility?" Brian demanded.

"I don't know," I said. "Familiars are smart, but they can't read. It's not like he'd be able to tell me what was on the sign at the storage facility, or whatever."

Actually, that was a flat-out lie. Because familiars helped their witches with their spells, they could read just as well as any human. Writing, on the other hand, wasn't something they could manage very well, since paws and claws weren't really designed to hold a pen or pencil.

However, that particular response clearly wasn't the answer Brian wanted to hear, because his finger tightened on the gun. "If he can't tell you where Darla took the box," he said, his tone soft, menacing, "then what good are either of you?"

Uh-oh. "He can show us," I said quickly. "Dogs are great at location. If he's been there once, he can take us there again."

"So, we're just supposed to drive aimlessly all over Chicago looking for a single storage facility?"

Put that way, the prospect did seem a little daunting. But....

"It wouldn't be aimless," I replied. "Milo would know where to take us. Anyway, how much do you want those videos?"

Once again, Brian was quiet for a moment. Then he said, "All right. You'd better not be lying to me."

"I'm not," I said, doing my best to look as guileless as possible.

"Wait there."

He stepped away from me, going to the suitcase he had sitting open on the folding stand next to the dresser. While it felt better to have a yard or so of distance between us, I couldn't relax too much, not while he had that menacing-looking gun trained on me the whole time.

Suitcase in hand, he commanded, "Open the door. Out in front is a black pickup truck. You and the dog get in when I unlock it."

"Okay," I replied, doing my best to seem thoroughly cowed.

I might have looked meek on the outside, but I knew that once Milo and I were free of that damn hotel room, it might be our only chance to make a break for it. We could shelter behind the truck while I busted out my broomstick and then take off. Yes, Brian would probably try to shoot at us, but that was where I had to hope the protection spells that surrounded both the dog and me would do their job until we were at a safe altitude where a bullet couldn't reach.

At least, that was the theory.

I put my hand on the doorknob and turned it. A quick look down at Milo and the slightest of nods, hoping he'd understand what I was trying to communicate, that he needed to follow my lead no matter what happened.

A very small flick of the dog's tail, one I guessed Brian didn't even notice. Then we were outside in the cool night air. Everything was as quiet as when I'd first gotten here a few minutes ago, telling me no one was stirring at the Sleepeasy Motel.

Well, no one except a witch, a familiar...and a murderer.

I spotted the truck, a big black Toyota Tundra. Still pretending that I was cooperating, I headed toward the passenger door. Thank God the truck was so big; it would do a good job of concealing what I planned to do next.

My left hand reached for the door handle as I

heard Brian engage the remote unlocking mechanism. That meant he was distracted...if only for a moment.

A moment was all I needed.

With my free hand, I reached into my purse and pulled out the broomstick, still in its disguise as a hairbrush.

Lovely broom
Save us from doom
Become your true shape
To help us escape!

The broomstick expanded into its true form. At the same time, I called to Milo, "Hop on!"

Still standing in front of the truck, Brian stared at us in shock...and then his eyes narrowed in anger just as quickly. He shoved the key fob in one pocket and the gun into the waistband of his pants, and snarled, "You're not the only one who's full of tricks!"

Fast as a blink—and before my brain could truly begin to comprehend what I was seeing—he shifted. Now there wasn't a man standing in front of me, but a thing, some horrible amalgam of man and animal that looked as though it had been cooked up in a truly deranged laboratory straight from a 1950s monster movie.

The thing...I couldn't really think of it as Brian

Alatorre anymore, not looking like that...landed on the hood of the truck with a thud that dented the metal, and came straight at me and Milo. My brain reacted much faster than my body, and I cried out,

Ball of fire
Make my enemy's pyre!

The fiery sphere flew straight at the creature. It snarled in fury and lifted a sinewy arm covered in patchy, pale brown fur, batting the fireball away. Luckily for the people who were still slumbering inside the Sleepeasy Motel, it went hurtling up and over the building, then landed with a clang inside something on the other side that I thought might be a dumpster.

Well, at least I didn't have to worry about burning down the place.

However, I definitely needed to worry about that monster ripping out my guts.

The fireball hadn't been too effective, but I hoped lightning bolts might be work better, if only because the spell I used to conjure them made it possible to throw more than one at a time.

Volley of light
Save me this night!

Bolts flew from my fingertips. The monster was

able to bat one of them away—it was positively chilling how he could do something like that, as though he was deflecting a volleyball someone had thrown at him—but the second one connected with his shoulder, knocking him back a few feet.

At the same time, he uttered a very human-sounding "ow!", which only made me wonder how much of the real Brian Alatorre was buried in there somewhere.

I didn't have time to ponder the conundrum, though, because Milo apparently had decided he needed to enter the fray as well, and lunged at the monster, teeth bared as he tore at the creature's leg.

My mind finally was able to process the realization that this was the thing which had attacked the dog several nights earlier. Not a tiger, not a bear, but something I'd never heard of before. Later—if I survived this encounter—maybe I'd have the opportunity to puzzle out exactly what Brian Alatorre was.

Now, though, I could only do my best to take advantage of the distraction Milo was providing.

The monster leaned down, claws on his lumpy, oversized hands extended. It was so easy to see how Milo had gotten those wounds on his throat and paws—and chillingly easy to imagine how those horrible talons might finish him off this time if I didn't intervene.

While the lightning bolts had hurt the creature

a little, they didn't seem to have slowed him down very much. I'd definitely have to do something about that.

Slow as a snail
So we can prevail!

All of a sudden, it was as though the monster was moving through the world's thickest molasses. Because he couldn't react, it was easy enough for Milo to charge in, teeth ripping at the thing's thigh.

Blood gushed out of the wound, bright red.

Did that mean the dog had hit the creature's femoral artery? Was its biology anything like that of the human being it had once been?

Apparently so, because it fell to the ground writhing, incoherent moans coming from its throat. Milo advanced—and so did I, grabbing the dog by his collar once I realized that the more blood the thing lost, the more human it looked.

A second later, it was once again Brian Alatorre.

An unconscious Brian, with blood gushing from the wound in his leg. Good thing he'd turned back into a man, though, because the door next to the room where he'd been staying opened, and a man and a woman who looked like they might be in their early twenties stuck their heads out, expressions irritated.

"Dude, some people are trying to sleep," the guy said. Then he seemed to focus on Brian's limp form, the blood that stained his cargo shorts.

"Call 9-1-1," I snapped, even as I knelt down and did my best to apply pressure to the wound. "But tell them to bring the police with them. This guy's wanted for murder in Chicago."

All right, that might have been a slight exaggeration, since the police there had absolutely no idea Brian Alatorre was the perpetrator they sought.

Still, my words had the desired effect, because the man's companion—who I realized had her phone out and was filming the entire incident—startled and then touched the screen, presumably dialing the emergency number.

And I grimly kept pressing down on Brian's leg, not knowing what else I could do. The shirt I was wearing didn't have enough extra fabric for me to tear off so I could create a makeshift tourniquet.

In the next moment, though, the girl with the phone came back, now holding a pillowcase.

"Use this."

I took it from her gratefully, tore off a strip, and tightened it around Brian's thigh just above the place Milo had savaged him. Then I looked over at the dog, realizing if the authorities arrived and figured out it was the dog who'd attacked the man lying on the ground in the parking lot, they'd take him away, euthanize him.

Not on my watch.

"Can you stay here with this man?" I asked. "I need to get the dog away. He was just protecting me, but...."

I let the words trail off, but the girl seemed to immediately understand, concern showing in her big brown eyes.

"Sure," she said. "Duncan and I will keep watch."

"Thank you," I replied. "Oh, and the guy's name is Brian Alatorre. He lives in Chicago, and he murdered a woman named Darla Fitzgerald."

The girl and her companion stared at me, wide-eyed, but I knew I couldn't hang around to answer any other questions, not with sirens already beginning to sound from far away, coming closer...fast.

"Time to go, Milo," I said, and grabbed my broom from the spot where I'd dropped it after Brian had gone on the attack.

I could only hope the girl who'd brought the pillowcase would think I'd been using the broomstick for self-defense.

To my relief, the dog seemed to realize this wasn't the right time for any questions, because he obediently followed me away from the parking lot and into the woods that backed up to the motel. As soon as we were safely hidden by the trees, he leaped onto the broomstick, sitting in front of me so I could wrap one arm around him and hold on.

Not the most comfortable position in the world, and yet I knew I'd hang on to him for dear life for as long as it took.

As the dog and I rose into the sky, an ambulance and several squad cars came screaming into the parking lot, sirens blaring, lights flashing. I knew they'd only be looking at the injured man who lay on the ground there, wouldn't be looking upward.

I didn't bother to waste time on my "look over there" spell.

Chapter 16

Fire in the Blood

It was past three o'clock by the time Milo and I landed in my moonlit garden. By that point, I was so tired I practically fell off my broom, although I held on long enough for the dog to make a more or less graceful dismount.

"Do you need a moment?" I asked the dog. After all, I had no idea whether Brian had been at all conscientious about allowing Milo to do his business at timely intervals.

I got a grateful nod in reply. "You can go inside, though," the dog told me. "Just leave the back door open."

That I could do. Broomstick in hand, I limped my way to the stoop and let myself in, leaving the door ajar for Milo's return. After I leaned the broom up against the pantry wall, I went to the refrigerator so I could pour myself some water from the pitcher I kept there.

As I replaced it, I noticed my hand was shaking.

No huge surprise, I supposed.

Milo came back in a moment later, and I closed the door and locked it. I'd left it unlocked plenty of times before, but after what I'd seen tonight, I wasn't taking any chances.

"All good?" I asked him.

In response, he wagged his tail.

"Good," I said. "Then let's go to bed."

I practically had to drag myself upstairs using the handrail, but eventually I made it. No wasting time to wash my face or even brush my teeth. Instead, I pretty much fell face first into bed, only pausing long enough to kick off my shoes and remove my jeans, and exchange my bloody shirt for a tank top I could sleep in. I'd have to remember to throw my clothes into the wash when I woke up the next morning.

That was basically my last conscious thought.

The sound of my phone ringing brought me back to the world. I blinked at the bright sunlight shimmering outside my bedroom window, then rolled over on one side to look at the clock on my bedside table.

Ten thirty-two.

Oh, no.

I was supposed to be at the shop over an hour ago.

Sitting bolt upright, I reached for my phone where I'd left it on the nightstand and had it at my ear without even stopping to look at the screen. "I am so sorry, Sage," I said. "I'll be in as quickly as I can."

"Who the hell is Sage?" a man's voice barked at me.

I blinked, realizing he sounded vaguely familiar. Then my brain cranked into gear, and I said, "Detective Adams?"

"Yes," he replied. His tone had shifted, and now he sounded almost amused. "Did I wake you?"

"Um, yes," I said. "I was up kind of late last night."

"So I gathered," he said dryly. "The New Hampshire state police had quite an interesting story to tell."

I was sure they did. "You don't say."

Now the detective chuckled. "I do say. I might have had a few choice words about the way you left the scene last night, but since you left us our perp neatly tied up with a bow, I suppose I can't complain too much. Mr. Alatorre wasn't too thrilled with you when we questioned him."

"So...." I blinked, wishing I had a cup of coffee sitting on my nightstand right then so I could take a bracing sip and unfog my brain a bit. "So, Brian Alatorre really is your guy?"

"Well, he hasn't been formally charged yet—holiday weekend—but I have no doubt that the D.A. will bring him up on charges of first-degree murder when Tuesday morning rolls around. Our forensics team picked up some DNA traces in Darla Fitzgerald's apartment that definitely didn't belong to her, but we didn't have a match until we had Alatorre in custody."

My slowly waking-up brain wondered why Brian hadn't turned back into the creature...whatever it was...and shredded his jailers to shreds. Was it because he'd been so badly wounded? Or maybe he could only shift into his monster form a few times a week?

Because I had absolutely no idea what was going on here, I couldn't begin to guess.

"He's very dangerous," I said.

"Oh, we know," Detective Adams replied, still sounding way too cheerful. I had to guess he was just relieved that a murder case which had seemed almost unsolvable had been cleared up for him in such an easy way. "He's still in the hospital—he lost a lot of blood—but we've got him shackled to the bed. He's not going anywhere."

Could the creature break those sorts of bonds?

Again, I didn't know. The thing was horribly strong, that much was obvious, but it could be wounded, could be brought down by a combination of magic and sheer canine bravery.

Also, I'd seen enough TV shows to know there were also probably armed cops watching Brian Alatorre, and he'd most likely be shot the second he started to shift. If a dog's bite could incapacitate him, then I had to believe a shot from a 9mm pistol —or whatever guns the police standing guard were carrying—would definitely be enough to prevent him from going anywhere.

"You may need to come back to Chicago to testify against him," Detective Adams continued.

"Um...sure," I replied. I didn't much like that prospect, but as long as I left Milo back here in Salem, it should be all right.

Of course, I might have a weensy little problem with that whole "tell the whole truth" part. There were lots of things about my interactions with Brian Alatorre that could never be uttered aloud in court, even if it meant perjuring myself.

Then again, even if I did tell the truth, I doubted anyone would believe me.

"Well, you have a good rest of your day," the detective said. "Just be prepared to hear from the D.A."

I said I'd be willing to help in whatever way necessary, and we ended the call there. As soon as I put down the phone, I raced to get in the shower and start prepping for my day.

Because no matter what else happened, I absolutely, positively had to be in the shop as soon as possible.

To my infinite relief, Sage wasn't too annoyed with me, even though the store was bustling with customers. I gave her a compressed version of what had happened the night before—in between helping our patrons, of course—and she sounded utterly shocked but couldn't ask me too many questions, thanks to all the mundies who'd flooded into the shop that bright Saturday morning on Memorial Day weekend.

Honestly, I was kind of glad I couldn't go into too many details. For one thing, I didn't have the answers to a lot of the questions she probably wanted to ask, and for another, I was still pretty wiped out from all my adventures the night before.

In a way, I was almost glad when I got a text from Noah a little before five.

> I am so sorry, but something's come up & I can't go out tonight. Rain check?

Sure. How about we wait until all
this holiday weekend insanity is
over with?

Perfect. I'll be in touch. Have a
nice, restful evening in!

Planning on it.

I ended the exchange with a wink emoji to
show him I wasn't upset about him canceling our
dinner plans at the last minute. Frankly, by that
point in the afternoon, I just wanted to go home,
put my feet up, and have Door Dash bring me
some Chinese food.

Even so, I couldn't help wondering what it was
that had prevented Noah from meeting me for
dinner.

Probably some kind of pet emergency, last-
minute surgery, something like that. After all, it
wasn't as though those sorts of crises waited to
happen conveniently during business hours.

My hopes for a quiet evening in were dashed
about a half hour after I got home, however. Just as
I was perusing the online menu at Hong Kong
King, wondering whether I was more in the mood
for orange chicken or cashew shrimp, my phone
rang.

A glance at the screen told me it was my
mother. I halfway wanted to ignore the call, but I

knew if I didn't pick up, she'd just keep trying until I did.

"Hi, Mom," I said.

"Emergency coven meeting at Grace's house," she replied.

I blinked. "A what?"

As far as I could remember, our little group of witches had never had an emergency meeting for anything.

"We need to talk to you," my mother said.

"Is this about Brian Alatorre?" I asked, mostly because I couldn't think of what else was going on that would make her sound so urgent.

"Yes," she said, "and that's all I want to say for now. Be there at seven."

She hung up then, while I stared down at my iPhone, puzzled. That whole exchange had seemed very unlike my mother. Usually, she was willing to chat endlessly until I was forced to break off the conversation.

None of this felt at all good to me.

Well, at least I didn't have to be at Grace's until seven. Since it was only a little past five-thirty, I still had time to order some food and eat before I had to leave.

I had a feeling I was going to need as much sustenance as possible to get me through that particular interrogation.

Because I knew tardiness would be frowned upon, I made sure to give myself plenty of time to get over to Grace's house, even though she only lived about ten minutes away. But Salem was choked with holiday travelers that weekend, and I knew they'd probably slow me down a lot more than I would have liked.

That proved to be the case, and I just barely squeaked in before the allotted time, pulling up to the curb in front of my destination at exactly seven o'clock. Several cars I recognized, including my mother's, were already parked at the curb and in the driveway.

Well, at least I was still being punctual, even if everyone else had already gotten here before me.

Grace opened the door when I knocked and ushered me inside, saying, "They're all waiting downstairs."

"Okay," I replied, then ventured, "Do you want to tell me what this is about?"

Her usually cheerful expression darkened. "Oh, you'll find out soon enough."

With those ominous words hanging in the air, I followed her down the stairs and into the basement room she used for her rituals. The other times I'd been here...because we tended to move things around so no one witch had to play hostess to every single ceremony...candles had flickered everywhere, and the air had been sweet with incense.

Tonight, though, the can lights installed in the ceiling had been turned on, making the deep green walls look almost garish. My mother—along with Valerie Monroe and Elise Figg and Tonya Willis—was already sitting there. Everyone in the group wore their regular everyday clothes, not the witchy gowns we preferred for casting magic, so whatever was going to take place tonight, it didn't seem as though it would be any kind of ceremony.

Grace sat down, and indicated that I should take the empty chair next to my mother. However, even though this was Grace's home and I'd just sort of expected that she'd be the one to lead the proceedings...whatever they turned out to be...it was actually Valerie Monroe who spoke first.

"I got a disturbing call from Izzy Halloran," she said, naming Sage's mother. "She said Sage told her about what happened to you in New Hampshire, Charity."

This news didn't surprise me as much as it might otherwise have. Sage and her mom were very close, and she'd probably wanted to relate my tale about the monster to get her mother's input on the subject. Maybe I should have tried to swear Sage to secrecy, but I didn't know how much good that would have done. As far as I could tell, my assistant told her mother pretty much everything.

And honestly, I never thought it mattered all that much, because whatever confidences the two of them might have shared, I knew they'd never go beyond our local witch community.

"And?" I said, still wondering what the point was of all this.

Valerie and my mother exchanged a glance. Although plumper than her granddaughter Stella, Valerie Monroe still shared a strong family resemblance, with her clear blue eyes and graceful features. She looked more troubled right now than I thought I'd ever seen her, though, telling me something was going on here that I couldn't quite figure out.

"Did you ever wonder, Charity, why it is that witches don't have male children?"

Wow, that question had come from straight out of left field. I shrugged, saying, "I suppose I thought magic only transfers through the female line, and it just sort of...self-selects...when we're conceived."

The other women in the room—all of them mothers, although Tonya Willis's daughter was grown and had moved to Burlington, Vermont—exchanged a loaded glance.

"I'm afraid it's not that simple," Valerie said. Her eyes, clear as a summer's day, met mine. "You see, when a witch has a male child, the magic manifests in him in a truly terrible way. That's why

Brian Alatorre was able to transform into the creature that attacked you and Milo."

For the longest second, I could only stare back at her. I was suddenly conscious of the thudding of my heart in my chest, of the quiet rustle of fabric as Elise Figg shifted in her chair and the long Indian-print skirt she was wearing swept against the floor.

"It's never supposed to happen this way," my mother put in. "We all cast spells as soon as we're pregnant, spells to guarantee that the child we're carrying is a girl. That way, we're making sure a creature like Brian Alatorre is never born."

"But he was born," I said, my voice flat.

"Yes," Valerie responded, now looking more sad than anything else. "We're still not sure how such a thing could have happened. Our best guess is that Lara Fitzgerald didn't realize she was carrying twins, and therefore the spells she cast wouldn't have affected the second fetus. Then, when Brian was born, she panicked and had him removed from the witch world so he would have no idea of what he might become."

I supposed that made some sense. But....

"She was taking an awful risk, wasn't she?" I ventured. "I mean, it doesn't seem very smart to dump a child like that on some unsuspecting mundie family."

"Yes, she was," Elise Figg put in. She had a light, pretty voice, one that seemed horribly unsuited for the discussion we were having. "I can only believe that her hormones were in such flux that she wasn't really thinking straight. Also, not every male child born to a witch has such a terrible talent."

"Just enough that the witch community knew we could never take such risks," Grace said. "Lara Fitzgerald must have been counting on the chance the boy would be safe...or, like Elise pointed out, she might not have been counting on anything at all, and was confused and acting on instinct. She definitely knew she could never raise him as her own."

No wonder Lara had looked so guilty, so abashed. Bad enough that she'd sent away one of her children to be raised by strangers. Far worse was the terrible reality that the baby she'd sent to a mundie household wasn't a cuckoo, but a fire-breathing dragon.

I couldn't quite keep the sharp note out of my voice as I asked, "And how come this is the first time I'm hearing about any of this?"

My mother spoke in reply, probably guessing it was her place to answer my pointed question. "Because you don't have children...and apparently aren't planning to have any." She paused there, and I worried for a moment that she was going to take the opportunity to needle me once again about my ticking biological clock. Apparently, she decided this wasn't the time to get personal, because she went on, "As soon as a witch becomes pregnant—or even sooner, if she lets the community know she's planning to have a child—we sit her down and explain the risks, and pass along the spell that will ensure she'll have a girl."

In most cases, this wouldn't have sounded like very good insurance. People got accidentally pregnant all the time, and often didn't even realize they were in that condition until things got far enough along. This angle prompted me to ask, "What happens if you don't cast the spells early enough?"

"Oh, as long as you start working the magic sometimes during the first half of the pregnancy, then it's fine," my mother assured me.

"Why not just cast a spell to make sure a witch's son is always born without magic?" I inquired next.

Grace and Elise Figg exchanged a weighted look at that question. Grace replied, "That was tried in the past. Let's just say it didn't work out at all well."

Apparently not. I could have pressed further on the subject, but it seemed pretty clear to me that the witches of generations past had been able to come up with only one solution to their terrible problem.

And that seemed to be that. Clearly, the precautions they'd come up with had worked for generations, or otherwise, we would have been knee-deep in shape-shifting witch boys.

"What will happen to Brian Alatorre now?" I asked then. "Obviously, the police don't have any idea about what they actually have in custody."

Valerie Monroe flickered a glance at Elise, who offered a nod so subtle, I wasn't sure I hadn't imagined it.

"He's wounded," Valerie said. "He won't be able to shift until he's mostly recovered."

Well, that was a bit of a relief, but still....

"And after that?"

My mother interceded then, her voice crisp. "He's a murderer and a monster, but he's not stupid. Shifting his form won't be enough to allow him to escape police custody, and it's certainly not in his best interests to allow the authorities to learn anything about his abilities. Being locked up in prison isn't much fun, but being sent to a lab to be studied would be much, much worse."

There was an angle I hadn't considered. But she was right. The second Brian Alatorre allowed anyone to learn he wasn't your ordinary garden-variety murderer, he'd be in a much deeper world of hurt.

"And as for those recordings he was going to exploit," Valerie went on, "we've already reached out to Lara Fitzgerald to let her know she needs to destroy them. I also contacted one of the members of the Witch Olympics committee to let her know the practice of filming the games needs to be banned completely. There's just far too much risk involved."

I definitely agreed with that particular point. It sounded to me as though the committee had been relying on the supposed solidarity among witches to make sure those recordings never fell into the wrong hands, but all it took was one disaffected person like Darla Fitzgerald to cause utter chaos.

"Normally, we wouldn't have had to say anything about all of this to you until you were ready to start a family," my mother put in. "But considering what you've experienced—what you've seen—we needed to let you know who...and what... Brian Alatorre really is."

About all I could do was nod. Although he was a terrible person and I was very, very glad he'd been caught, I also couldn't quite hold back a sneaking bit of pity for the man. He hadn't asked to be born what he was, and he'd certainly never had anyone around who could help him try to come to terms with the twisted magic that lived inside him.

"I'm glad," I said. "I mean, I'm not glad it happened, but I'm definitely glad that part of the mystery has been cleared up."

"So are we," Valerie replied. "And I know I speak for all of us when I say we sincerely hope nothing like this ever happens again."

"Same here," I said, in heartfelt tones.

My mother got up from her chair, and came over and gave me a hug. "You've had a rough couple of days, sweetie. Go home and try to get some rest. Everything will look better tomorrow."

I sincerely hoped so. After hugging her back, I also stood up. "Thank you for telling me," I said, addressing all the witches in the room.

"You needed to know," Tonya said, speaking for the first time. "But now it's time for you to put this behind you and get on with your life."

A life that would, I hope, be mercifully free of shape-changing male witches and secrets and lies.

"Amen to that," I remarked, and everyone chuckled.

Driving home that night, I did feel a little better. Not all the way, because it was truly frightening to think that a male child born of a witch could carry the burden of such a horrible birthright, but at least now I knew the truth.

I slept better than I'd expected to that night, and woke up at a reasonable time and was there to open the shop the next morning, just like I was supposed to. To tell the truth, I'd almost called Sage and told her I'd changed my mind about opening on Sunday at all, but that would have been the coward's way out. We'd have Monday off, and that should be good enough. At least we only had to work three days of this holiday weekend and not four.

However, that peace of mind only lasted until a little before two in the afternoon, when I got another call from Detective Adams.

"I didn't think I'd hear from you again so soon," I said, half joking. I also wondered whether the man ever got a day off.

"He's gone," he said brusquely, and I frowned.

"Who's gone?"

"Brian Alatorre. He died in his sleep last night."

For the longest second, I just stood there, phone pressed to my ear. My brain didn't quite want to absorb the information it had just received.

Then, since I could tell the detective was waiting for me to make some kind of reply, I managed to ask, "What happened?"

"The doctors don't know for sure. Probably an aneurysm. Anyway, I just wanted to let you know so you wouldn't have to worry about coming back to Chicago to testify against him. Have a good day."

Then he ended the call, and I stood there for a moment, staring blankly down at the phone in my hand.

"Do you have anything for arthritis?" a woman with dyed hair even redder than mine and bright pink sunglasses asked.

I blinked, taking a second to focus on the here and now. "Um...sure. Let me show you."

But even as I led the woman over to the shelf that contained the tinctures she wanted, my brain was going a mile a minute. Brian Alatorre's death seemed awfully suspicious...and convenient. I thought of the glance Valerie had sent Elise, and the barely perceptible nod she'd gotten in return.

Was Elise somehow responsible for the "aneurysm" Detective Adams had mentioned? I'd never heard of her practicing that sort of magic— you had to be extremely careful about working anything dark, anything that caused harm, in case it rebounded on you—but I supposed it wasn't the sort of thing you'd want to announce on a street corner even if you did dabble in the black arts.

Problem was, I doubted Elise would give me a straight answer if I asked her point-blank whether she had anything to do with Brian Alatorre's untimely death.

Protecting the witch community was para-mount. If Valerie and Elise and Tonya—and yes, my mother—had decided they couldn't take the risk of him spilling the beans, then I could see how they might have chosen a quiet death for the man, thinking it was probably better than he deserved.

Darla Fitzgerald's death hadn't been anywhere as painless, that's for sure.

To my relief, the customer I was helping didn't

need any other assistance after I'd pointed her in the direction of the tinctures she wanted, so I was able to head back to the counter and do my best to focus on ringing up people's purchases. Sage, seeming to sense I was preoccupied, took over most of the customer service duties in terms of answering questions or directing people to the shelves that contained the items they needed, so I could handle the mostly mindless task of taking payments from our patrons.

At last, five o'clock rolled around, and we shooed the last of the customers out of the store before I locked the door, gladder than ever that I'd decided to close the shop on Monday. Another day like this, and I would've needed a week to recover.

"Well, that's that," Sage said after she turned off the "Open" sign in the front window. "Any big plans for tomorrow?"

"Besides sleeping for ten hours?" I replied, only halfway joking.

She grinned. "Yeah, you did seem kind of out of it today. But I can see why."

You don't know the half of it, I thought, although I only shrugged in response to Sage's comment. There was no way in the world I could tell my assistant that I suspected Elise Figg of sending a nasty little spell winging Brian Alatorre's way, something that would ensure he never told anyone about the secret society of witches living right under their noses. I didn't have any proof, only the realization that the whole thing had been *way* too convenient.

The two of us headed out back, said goodbye and that we'd see each other on Tuesday, and got into our respective vehicles. As I drove home, I found myself increasingly tense, rather than glad I'd have a whole day off to recuperate.

It seemed strange that I hadn't heard from Noah all day. Maybe he'd simply realized I was going to be crazy-busy and so didn't want to bother me at work, but you'd think he at least would have sent me a quick text to try to reschedule our date.

He's just giving you space, I told myself. *He'll call you tomorrow when he knows you're not working.*

That explanation sounded reasonable enough. But....

Something made me turn off onto Washington Street, heading toward Noah's house rather than my own home. I knew Milo was waiting for me, but now that Brian was no longer a threat, the dog and I had both decided it was better for him to stay at my place rather than come into work. The house and the garden were warded, and Milo knew not to leave the property, so I'd left the back door partway open in order to allow him to go in and out as he pleased.

Because he wouldn't have to wait for me to let him out, I guessed I didn't see the problem in making a teeny little detour.

A red Volvo SUV I didn't recognize was parked in Noah's driveway. I frowned at it, even as I told myself he wasn't a hermit and had made some friends here in Salem, although obviously, his circle wasn't nearly as big as mine. It seemed perfectly plausible that he might be relaxing and watching a ballgame with a friend, maybe getting ready to barbecue when it got a little later.

Because the driveway was occupied, I had to pull up to the curb. As I got out, I reflected this was probably a huge mistake. For one thing, I was feeling frazzled and probably looked it, and for another, I didn't want to come off as some kind of crazy stalker girlfriend or something.

Not that we'd been together long enough for me to even consider myself Noah's girlfriend.

But I was here, and if he'd somehow spotted me as I parked, it would look even weirder for me to get back in my Discovery and head home. No, I'd just manufacture some white lie about Milo, and try to figure out where the land lay after I was safely back at the house.

When I rang the doorbell, though, it wasn't Noah who answered it.

No, it was a woman I'd never seen before, around my age or maybe a little older, with shoulder-length blonde hair and pretty, regular features. She stared at me, baffled, then said, "Can I help you?"

"Is Noah home?" I asked, and quickly added, "He's been taking care of my dog."

Her head tilted, and a small frown pulled at her perfectly groomed brows. "Shouldn't you be taking your dog to an emergency vet instead of coming to Noah's house?"

A perfectly valid response, I supposed, and yet something about her tone rankled. I placed my hands on my hips and said, "And who are you?"

She smiled then, looking much more cheerful. "I'm Shelby Howard.

"I'm Noah's fiancée."

~

Charity's adventures continue in *Cauldrons and Cats.*

Also by Christine Pope

FAMILIAR SPIRITS

(Cozy Fantasy/Romance)

Spells and Spaniels

Cauldrons and Cats

Hexes and Hedgehogs

Charms and Chihuahuas

LATTES AND LEVITATION

(Cozy Mystery/Paranormal Romance)

Caffeine Before Curses

Muffins After Magic

Pastries and Prophecies

Eclairs and Ectoplasm

Sugar Skulls and Specters

UNEXPECTED MAGIC*

(Urban Fantasy/Paranormal Romance)

Found Objects

Finders, Keepers

Lost and Found

Finding Destiny

HEDGEWITCH FOR HIRE

(Cozy Mystery/Paranormal Romance)

Grave Mistake

Social Medium

Household Demons

Perpetual Potion

Jingle Spells

Wandering Monsters

Uninvited Ghosts

Prophet Motive

Ballroom Bits

THE WITCHES OF WHEELER PARK*

(Paranormal Romance)

Storm Born

Thunder Road

Winds of Change

Mind Games

A Wheeler Park Christmas

Blood Ties

Healing Hands

Wishful Thinking

Smoke and Mirrors

MISS PRIMM'S ACADEMY FOR WAYWARD
WITCHES*

(Fantasy/Academy Romance)

Misspelled

Dispelled

Expelled

PROJECT DEMON HUNTERS*

(Paranormal Romance)

Unquiet Souls

Unbound Spirits

Unholy Ground

Unseen Voices

Unmarked Graves

Unbroken Vows

THE DEVIL YOU KNOW*

(Paranormal Romance)

Sympathy for the Devil

Charmed, I'm Sure

A Wing and a Prayer

Wish Upon a Star

THE WITCHES OF CANYON ROAD*

(Paranormal Romance)

Hidden Gifts

Darker Paths

Mysterious Ways

A Canyon Road Christmas

Demon Born

An Ill Wind

Higher Ground

Haunted Hearts

THE WITCHES OF CLEOPATRA HILL*

(Paranormal Romance)

Darkangel

Darknight

Darkmoon

Sympathetic Magic

Protector

Spellbound

A Cleopatra Hill Christmas

Impractical Magic

Strange Magic

The Arrangement

Defender

Bad Blood

Deep Magic

Darktide

THE DJINN WARS*

(Paranormal Romance)

Chosen

Taken

Fallen

Broken

Forsaken

Forbidden

Awoken

Illuminated

Stolen

Forgotten

Driven

Unspoken

THE WATCHERS TRILOGY*

(Paranormal Romance)

Falling Dark

Dead of Night

Rising Dawn

THE SEDONA FILES*

(Paranormal/Science Fiction Romance)

Bad Vibrations

Desert Hearts

Angel Fire

Star Crossed

Falling Angels

Enemy Mine

The Gaia Gambit

The Mandala Maneuver

The Titan Trap

The Zhore Deception

The Refugee Ruse

STANDALONE TITLES

Hearts on Fire (Paranormal Romance)

Taking Dictation (Contemporary Romance)

Golden Heart (Gaslight Fantasy Romance)

Night Music: A Modern Reimagining of The Phantom
of the Opera (Contemporary Romance)

Ghost Dance: A Sequel to Gaston Leroux's The
Phantom of the Opera (Historical Mystery/Romance)

Flight Before Christmas (Fantasy Romance)

* Indicates a completed series

About the Author

USA Today bestselling author Christine Pope has been writing stories ever since she commandeered her family's Smith-Corona typewriter back in grade school. Her work includes paranormal romance, cozy paranormal mystery, and urban fantasy, among others. She makes her home in beautiful Santa Fe, New Mexico.

Christine Pope on the Web:
www.christinepope.com

facebook.com/ChristinePopeAuthor
pinterest.com/ChristineJPope
bookbub.com/authors/christine-pope

www.ingramcontent.com/pod-product-compliance
Lightning Source LLC
Chambersburg PA
CBHW020408260626

47156CB00007B/2290